3²⁵

FAR BEYOND
THE STARS

	DATE DUE	

STAR TREK
DEEP SPACE NINE®

FAR BEYOND
THE STARS

A novel by
STEVE BARNES

Based on
FAR BEYOND THE STARS

Teleplay by
**IRA STEVEN BEHR &
HANS BEIMLER**

Story by
MARC SCOTT ZICREE

POCKET BOOKS
New York   London   Toronto   Sydney   Tokyo   Singapore

An *Original* Publication of POCKET BOOKS

POCKET BOOKS, a division of Simon & Schuster Inc.
1230 Avenue of the Americas, New York, NY 10020

This book is published by Pocket Books, a division of Simon & Schuster Inc., under exclusive license from Paramount Pictures.

ISBN: 0-671-02430-2

First Pocket Books printing April 1998

10 9 8 7 6 5 4 3 2 1

POCKET and colophon are registered trademarks of Simon & Schuster Inc.

Printed in the U.S.A.

FAR BEYOND
THE STARS

CHAPTER
1

FROM THIS FAR PERSPECTIVE, the planet Bajor was a misty, radiant opal, beautiful as a star, peaceful as the long-lost memories of the womb. Alone in her shuttle pod, Major Kira soared high above the surface of her home world, aching with the irony of that apparent quietude. Once, Bajor might have known only harmony—but not in Kira's time, nor her parents', nor her grandparents'. War had torn the planet apart for far too many bloody years. But the planet of her birth, a gentle haze of oceans even now receding to a glittering demistar, was still the most beautiful place that Kira could ever dream of.

The shuttle's engines hummed beneath her. Escape from Bajor's gravity was the only tricky part of the entire journey: she could begin to relax and slip into one of the vexing contemplations that often plagued her at this point. This time, her mind took a particularly troublesome turn: What small shifts in circumstance might have given Bajor a greater chance at peace?

Bajor was too close to the Cardassian border, a tempting prize, too wealthy by far, whether wealth was measured in material or spiritual values. That last, perhaps, was what had proved her undoing. To have nothing and be unprepared for the predators in the world, was one thing. But to be rich and still unable to defend oneself seemed to motivate not merely greed, but anger.

Her reflection gleamed faintly in the shuttle's windows. She watched her hands play across the controls. Major Kira was still attractive, and she would be for many years to come. She had dedicated her life to service, a decision it was too late to change, or turn back from. Like too many, she had both the gift and the curse of knowing her place in the world. A gift because it removes uncertainty. A curse because it sometimes eliminates wonder.

She was not the only one possessing this barbed gift. Another, she knew, understood his place in the world. And although they had experienced difficulties and differences, of all of the people who worked and lived in the place called *Deep Space Nine,* Benjamin Sisko was perhaps closest to a brother. He knew what it was to find his place in the world. He grasped both the positive and negative aspects of that understanding, the way in which it was both gift and curse.

Benjamin Sisko. The man to whom she would have to relay her data, information too precious to be trusted to any transmitted message, no matter how secure. Information which would add to his already massive load of stress.

The shuttle trip between Bajor and DS9 lasts approximately three hours. Originally, DS9 was a Cardassian mining station built in orbit above the planet Bajor during the Cardassian occupation. Constructed in 2351, initially called *Terok Nor,* DS9 was intended to exploit Bajor's rich uridium deposits. The Cardassians retained control of the station until 2369, when they relinquished their claim on Bajor and retreated from the region. Now administered by the Federation, the station fell under the jurisdiction of the Bajoran government and was subject to its laws.

During much of the travel time between Bajor and the station, Major Kira allowed herself to fall into a state very close to a trance. If she could just quiet her mind, this portion of the trip could be quite soothing. There were so many incredible sights, so much for her eyes to feast on—even more so since the discovery of the wormhole. The Bajoran wormhole was an invisible bridge between worlds, inhabited by creatures which her people referred to as the Prophets. The Prophets, who had supplied spiritual governance to the Bajorans over the years, now linked the Bajor system to the distant Gamma Quadrant.

This remarkable place, in which ordinary rules of consciousness were sometimes nullified, was the spot to which *Deep Space Nine* had been towed. As Kira drew nearer the station, she felt herself shifting from one way of being to another, one mode of operation to another. From contemplative wanderer to first officer.

Home to about three hundred permanent staff,

DS9's immense docking ring was the most remarkable aspect of the structure. When approached from the side its docking pylons resembled nothing so much as a glittering pair of parentheses linked by a central docking ring. With the ease of long practice, she glided her shuttle into the docking port. There was no need for her to rely on one of the upper or lower docking pylons, the large, skeletal-looking arms which extended vertically from the horizontal docking ring.

The actions that followed she performed on pure autopilot. There was no sense of challenge in this, only an overwhelming concern for the man that she called friend, and the knowledge that she bore not one, but two pieces of evil news. It was more than any man should be forced to bear. It might be . . . what was the Earth expression? "The straw that broke the camel's back"?

CHAPTER 2

BENJAMIN SISKO'S OFFICE was spare and functional, as uncomplicated as he could make it, a place for thought and consideration, not feeling. It had a magnificent view, the majesty of an infinite starscape, occasionally overshadowed by the blossoming of the Bajoran wormhole. There were times when he could appreciate its beauty, and others when he thought only of the beings deep within it, the mysterious Prophets who had shown him so much, had brought him so close to both madness and some total, ineffable understanding. He couldn't help the fact that his emotions toward the wormhole and its residents vacillated. Was it a spiritual font, from which had blossomed a religion of depth and grace? Or was it merely a trade route, bringing resources and sorely needed industry to a beleaguered people? Was it a thing of beauty? An anomaly created by beings beyond human understanding?

No matter how he chose to consider it, there were aspects which eluded him. Ultimately, he was left with his own feelings and perceptions, as were all men. Ultimately, he was left with himself. He fought to collect his thoughts, to center his emotions. For months now, negotiations had raged between the Federation and the Bajorans. There were a dozen different volatile issues at stake, and most of them had been resolved. There were too many lives at stake, too much that could go wrong, too many different factions that wanted to pull the votes this way or that.

Too many lives in the balance. He needed all of his strength focused on one duty, one concern at a time, and unfortunately, that vital attention had been split by the current emergency.

Benjamin Sisko was a tall, dark man, shaven-headed, with a sparse goatee and mustache that framed a face of unusual intelligence. His ancestors had come from both Africa and Europe, those bloodlines meeting in America, on Earth, centuries before. That was many light-years away in other, simpler times. None of his ancestors had held such responsibility in their hands. Few men or women ever bear that curse, or receive that gift.

He had slept poorly that night, as he had for the previous week. He could trace his insomnia to a central event: mining negotiations reaching a critical phase. He looked forward to his meeting with Major Kira more than he let himself consciously admit. Others under his command, friends, comrades, and subordinates, had noticed that his nerves were running a little raw. Even his beloved son, Jake, had noticed that their weekly gravball match hadn't been as much fun as usual. Usually, if the boy upped his skill or competitive drive a notch, his father exalted in it. This time, Jake's exceptional play triggered something in Benjamin Sisko just too damned close to anger, a flash of resentment that had to be more fatigue than real jealousy.

But things were almost at a close now: soon, the ore would start to flow, and with it the exchange of arts and commerce. Things would not just be back to normal—they might well be more stable than at any time since he had taken control of the station, five long years before.

At the most critical junction, another, more personal blow had struck. But perhaps, just perhaps, Major Kira bore good tidings . . .

With a barely audible shush, the door to his office opened, and she appeared. Sisko rose from his desk smiling. "Major," he began. "I heard that your shuttle had docked. I can't tell you how happy I am that—," something in her face told him that his celebration was premature.

She handed him the flat wedge of a Personal Access Display Device. He knew that it would be in an encoded, single-use mode, designed for highly confidential information between high-security personnel. This was not good.

"Kira?"

"I don't feel comfortable, sir—I don't want any words or thoughts to be misinterpreted because of my own inability to communicate. Please. Just activate the padd."

Sisko weighed the device thoughtfully, and then spoke to it. "Captain Benjamin Sisko," he said finally. He pressed his palm against its surface. It glowed briefly, reading a dozen different factors from his body chemistry, voice, and physiognomy. It unlocked.

One at a time, the row of three red lights along the top of the black wedge winked on. A rectangular screen cleared and the recorded image of a silver-robed Bajoran appeared.

"Shakaar," Sisko said soberly.

"Captain Sisko," Shakaar said, seeming to actually respond to his presence. "We have considered the proposals brought before us, and wish to make decisions which are considerate of all sides of this matter, so as to avoid conflict. While most components of the proposed treaty are agreed to, we must, for the time being, consider the fourth codicil unsatisfactory. We hope that you will be able to communicate our wish for fair treatment of all involved in this most delicate matter."

There it was, the blow that he had feared, and darkly expected. There it was, hidden behind the polite Bajoran diplomatic speech, the oblique phrasing. All was well, save for the "fourth codicil."

Benjamin Sisko rose from behind his desk, something like a red-tinged cloud of black ink raging behind his eyes. His fingers gripped the padd as if he wanted to crush it.

Were they mad? Didn't they understand what was at stake here? "How can the First Minister refuse to allow Federation mining operations on Bajor?"

Damn! It was back to first base now—months of effort and wheedling, months of careful concessions and discreet exchanges, all blown to hell by that damned phrase.

Kira's voice came to him as if from a distance, the voice of reason in the midst of his storm. "Shakaar didn't make this decision alone," she said reasonably. "The entire Council voted it down."

"Is that supposed to make me feel better?" he asked bitterly. The Federation had spent resources, time and precious lives protecting the Bajorans, and reciprocity was supposedly the soul of politics. The pressure on him, from the Federation and from the Dominion, was an almost palpable thing. Sometimes he felt as if the air itself were slowly turning into soup. He fought to calm his voice. *You're Benjamin Sisko,* he said to himself. *Be who you are.* "Your planet has many, many things which we hold precious, but chief among them is the fact that Bajor is rich in uridium ore. The Federation needs that ore to rebuild its fleet."

He hoped that he wouldn't need to raise his voice. The threat of war, after so many years of peace, was a very real thing once again. As a young man he had longed for active service. But raising a son changed so many things. What was glorious adventure for a single man was . . . well, it was a menace to the harmony and safety of a home. Home. That was, after all, what

DS9 meant to him now, and he hated to see anything threaten that. The possibility of Bajor closing its doors did just that.

War looms on the horizon, and if the Federation became desperate enough, they would take what they need. I will be the instrument of that, and all of the time spent developing delicate relationships with your culture will be gone in an instant.

"The Emissary told Bajor to stay out of the war," Kira said. "They're only doing what you told them to do."

By invoking the honorific bestowed upon Sisko by the Prophets, Kira was attempting to enlist DS9's commander as Bajor's ally in the negotiation. And that he couldn't allow her to do. "I know," he said, "but now the Emissary is telling them to allow the Federation to move forward with this mining operation."

Kira could not be so easily dissuaded. Her logic was severe. "No," she said. "This request isn't coming from the Emissary—it's coming from a Starfleet Captain."

He groaned. It was hair-splitting, expertly accomplished, and he was hoist on his own petard. "And Bajor would rather listen to the Emissary."

There it was again. What was real? What was right? He could look at himself in the mirror and see so many different Benjamin Siskos. Father, Captain, diplomat and . . . visionary?

She might have read his mind. "Can you blame them?" Kira's voice was not unkind. "The Emissary speaks for the Prophets."

And there, certainly, was truth. The immortal Prophets were timeless beings of staggering power. They lived in, and had created the Bajoran wormhole. They had gifted the Bajorans with the sacred Orbs, which were the basis for all of their religion and much of their culture. When the Prophets chose Benjamin Sisko as the Emissary, it elevated him from a mere Starfleet Captain to a voice of wisdom and experience. But when he spoke in his role as . . . well, Federation mouthpiece, the Bajorans had no such obligation to listen.

It was tearing him apart. What was right for the Federation? What was right for the Bajorans?

And what was right for Benjamin Sisko?

Sisko sank back into his chair, fingers massaging his temples. That headache, the steady throbbing, was back again. There now seemed no place to hide from it.

"All I know is that if the Federation can't count on Bajor . . ." he momentarily lost the thread of his words. He closed his eyes, relieved to be left in darkness. The last thing that he saw before he closed them was the face of Major Kira, filled with concern. Darkness. What to do? Who was he at this moment? Diplomat? Federation officer? Emissary? Father to his son?

Or just Benjamin Sisko, a man feeling weary and too damned pressured. "Sometimes . . ." he said, and for the moment he was speaking more to himself than to Kira. "It all seems so . . . overwhelming. No matter what I do, no matter how many fires I put out, another one erupts somewhere else." He paused. "Tell me, Nerys, when did everything get so grim?" He turned to Major Kira, a scintilla of hope still alive within him. "On the other matter. Is there any word . . . ?"

She sighed heavily. "I'm sorry to bear ill tidings twice, sir. The *Defiant* searched the quadrant for almost six hours, but found no sign of survivors."

"I don't believe this," he finally managed to say. "It just isn't right." He paused, collecting himself. "The *Cortez* was a fine ship."

"You knew Captain Swofford a long time," Kira said sympathetically.

Too long. Benjamin Sisko was not a man who made friends easily. The loss of one felt like a small, personal death. "I introduced him to his wife," he said, more to himself than Kira.

"Patrolling the Cardassian border is getting more and more hazardous," she said. "You never know when you're going to run into a squadron of Jem'Hadar fighters."

He shook his head in disgust. "Well. I guess we popped the champagne corks too soon."

"Sir?"

"Everyone thought the war was over when we retook the station and pushed the Dominion back into Cardassian space."

"I never believed that." Kira kept her voice carefully neutral. "And neither did you."

"A lot of good that did the four hundred people on the *Cortez*." He could imagine the *Cortez* too clearly, hulls shredding beneath the terrible energy assault, the silent screams of a crew trapped between fire and vacuum. An infinite moment of mind-freezing pain and horror . . .

And then peace.

God help him, at this moment, he envied them.

Major Kira watched her friend and commander, his knuckles whitening as he ground them against his desk. She felt helpless, wished that she could reach out and comfort him, but knew that the gesture would be improper, and worse than useless. Instead, she excused herself, and left the room.

On the way into the hall, she passed a tall, graying man who nodded his greeting—and hope blossomed within her. His dark, intelligent eyes had seen so very much of life. This was the one person from whom Benjamin might accept comfort—his father, Joseph Sisko. Hope blossomed within her.

A resident of distant Earth, Joseph Sisko couldn't have picked a worse time for a personal visit—or a better one—for a mission of spiritual and emotional support. She forced a smile to her face. "Mister Sisko," she said. "So, how do you like our station so far?"

"It certainly is big," he said. The man had a talent for understatement.

She breathed a sigh of relief as he headed into his son's quarters. Benjamin Sisko's emotional health now rested in the very best hands imaginable.

The pounding in Sisko's ears, the darkness that loomed every time he closed his eyes had swarmed closer to the surface. He blinked hard as his father entered his chamber—he needed to collect himself. He didn't want Joseph to worry.

Too late—his father was already worried. "I heard about Quentin Swofford," the older man said. "I'm sorry."

Through some odd persistence of vision, the speckles of light remained in Sisko's view even when he tried to focus. They swarmed around his father, diffracting the light a bit. "Look, Dad . . . I know I haven't been very good company the last few days."

Joseph Sisko wouldn't even let his son begin the trip down that morose path. "I didn't come here to be entertained. I came to see you and Jake."

"You picked an interesting time to take your first trip away from Earth."

His father's laughter was deep and genuine. "Well, I figured it was now or never. Besides, I've been worried about you. Last couple of times we've talked . . . it seemed like the weight of the entire Alpha Quadrant was on your shoulders."

Sisko could understand *that*. "Sometimes it feels that way." He struggled to form the next words—they just didn't want to emerge. "Dad . . . I'm not sure . . ."

"Just say it, Son."

Benjamin sighed. "I just don't know how many friends I can lose. Every time I think I've achieved a real victory, something like this happens and it all turns to ashes." There, he had said it, and although a weight had been lifted thereby, he also felt hollowed out.

"So what do you want to do?" his father asked gently.

"Maybe it's time for me to step down," Benjamin said. "Let someone else make the tough calls."

The two men, father and son, regarded each other for a long moment. The older man was the first to speak. "I see," he said, and then paused. "Well, no one's indispensable, Son. Not even you. Whatever decision you make, I'll support it." He paused again, and the slightest of thoughtful smiles curled his lips. "Of course, if Quentin Swofford was here . . . I'd bet he'd have a few things to say to you."

Sisko thumped his fist on the desk. "But he's not here . . . is he? That's the whole point."

Joseph nodded. "I'd say you have some thinking to do . . . and I've got a dinner date with my grandson, so I'll let you get to it."

The light disturbance weakened until Sisko thought it had disappeared . . . then suddenly strengthened again. Sisko saw his father, but the room around him shimmered. Everything was normal, and yet . . .

Something just behind him, in the hall. A man sauntered past. He seemed to be purposeful, calm, directed. In fact, there was nothing unusual about him, with the exclusion of the fact that he wore a gray flannel suit. Sisko blinked hard. No, he was right. It wasn't Cardassian silk, or one of the Vulcan demicottons which sometimes resembled some of the older earth fabrics. He looked as if he had stepped out of the holosuite, still cloaked in fantasy.

"Did you see that man?" he asked, annoyed that

the bizarre image had disrupted his train of thought. "Who was that?"

"Who?" Joseph spun about. Sisko was up in a moment, and crossed to the door before his father could gather his wits.

Sisko looked out at Operations, and saw only the familiar faces of Dax, Kira, O'Brien and a half a dozen other crew members, at their stations, holding down the fort as always. There were scanners and communications equipment and weapons controls, but no sign of what looked very much like a mid-20th-century conservative American dress style. He hardly noticed when Joseph Sisko appeared behind him.

"Where did he go?" Sisko asked, baffled.

His father was no less confused. "Who?"

"The man who just walked by my door."

Dax glanced at Kira, growing more concerned now. "I didn't see anyone," she said.

Sisko rubbed his left fingers against his temples. "He . . . was wearing a gray suit of some kind."

"Sorry, Captain," Dax said. "We must have missed him."

Sisko saw in their faces that they were willing to accept this answer—that someone might have walked right through their midst, right past their captain's office, and that they hadn't seen this odd intruder. They were willing to accept the possibility but they didn't believe it. And neither did he.

"I could've sworn," he began, then let his voice trail off. More than anyone in the room, he was achingly aware of just how lame that sounded. They were staring openly now, and he didn't blame them a bit.

With difficulty, he managed to force a smile to his lips. "Never mind," he said to his father. He turned to Dax. "If you need me, Old Man, I'll be with Kasidy."

Dax watched him carefully. They had known each other far too long—Dax understood the implication between his words. *I need to talk, but not now, and not in front of the crew.*

Sisko crossed to the turbolift, and it shushed open for him. "Habitat Ring," he said. "Level Ten, Section Four."

As it sank out of sight, the others glanced significantly at Kira. "What was *that* all about?" O'Brien asked. His ordinarily ruddy face was even darker than usual. This was a time of stress for all of them, and no time to doubt the health or sanity of their captain.

"I'm not entirely sure," she said. "But I promise I'll check into it. I'll keep you posted. Back to work."

"Yes, Sir."

CHAPTER
3

BENJAMIN SISKO SWORE his stomach floated up into his throat as the turbolift sank. He knew that wasn't possible—there was really no perceptible sense of motion in any of the lifts. Still, something like tiny bubbles danced in the back of his head. Maybe he had contracted that Vulcan flu that was going around. It was very rare for humans to catch it, but when they did, it could be exceptionally severe. *Nothing to sneeze at,* he said to himself and managed to chuckle. If he could make a joke, even one as slight as that, perhaps all was not lost.

Still, a trip to the infirmary might well be in line.

On the other hand, in all probability it was just the stress, mounting steadily now as it had for days. He needed rest of one kind or another. If stress was the disease, he knew the cure any compassionate doctor would prescribe.

In the five years since assuming command of DS9, he had been involved with several women. Only one had claimed his heart, the beautiful and brilliant Kasidy Yates. There had been long years when he had feared that no one would ever be able to take the place of his beloved wife Jennifer. That had been accurate—no one could. But the human heart is a strange thing. It does not heal so much as grow *around* the hurt. Kasidy had helped him to heal, and for that, as well as the warmth and joy she brought him, he loved her.

She stood with her back turned to him as he approached her door, dictating something softly into her padd. Probably one of the last-minute notes that seemed to bubble up from her unconscious only when she had turned her conscious attention elsewhere.

Sisko slid behind her and slipped his arms around her waist, reveling in the soft strong curves, in the soft sweet scent of her hair-oil. She stiffened for a moment and then relaxed into his embrace, leaning back against him.

"Mmmm, Odo," she said. "If Benjamin catches us—"

In spite of his dark mood, he managed a chuckle. He spun her in his arms.

Kasidy's eyes widened in mock surprise. "Why— why, Ben! I was kidding of course—"

She locked her arms around his neck, and cocked her head sideways. "Really, I was," she said.

"I'm not sure I should believe you," he said. Her eyes twinkled, and her door opened behind them.

"I think that if you'll step into my quarters," she said mischievously, "I could prove my sincerity."

"As captain of this station," Sisko was surprised to hear the husk in his voice, to feel the sudden tension in his body, surprised and delighted at Kasidy's infinite ability to take him out of himself. For the millionth time, he gave thanks that she was his. "It is my obligation to investigate all charges made by one crewman against another. You should be given a chance to defend yourself."

"All rise," she said. Taking his hand, she led him into the welcoming darkness. "Court is now in session."

CHAPTER
4

TIME PASSES TOO QUICKLY, Sisko thought. *I need a week of this, of just quiet time. Why can't someone synthesize time?*

They stood outside her room, peaceful and content just to touch each other gently and share a few quiet moments. Kasidy's fingers smoothed nonexistent wrinkles from his uniform. Her eyes were liquid gold, and he remembered clearly, only minutes before, when they had boiled with heat for him. His troubles seemed very far away.

He leaned forward and kissed her again. She returned it enthusiastically and then laid her fingers delicately on his collar, pushing him back.

"Hungry?" he asked.

"I can eat," she said, eyes half lidded.

He playfully pulled her back toward the room, but

she laughed and tugged him down the hall. "Down, boy," she said.

"You're going to have to stop feeding me straight lines," Sisko said.

"We have time. I'm not scheduled to leave 'til late this evening."

"Good news and bad news. I was hoping that we might be able to get away for a little holodeck vacation. Until the Federation reacts to the latest Bajoran proposal, I'm in limbo." Sudden irritation stole a bit of the contentment from his mood. "Aren't there any other freighter captains the Bajoran Commerce Ministry can call on?"

"Sure, but these days, most of them prefer to stay close to Bajor."

He growled, but couldn't pretend not to understand. "I have to admit I'm worried about you."

Her smile was so bright, as if she was discussing the possibility of a picnic on the beach, not a potential life and death encounter. "Ben—don't mother me. I'm not taking my ship anywhere near the Cardassian border."

"I realize that. But the Dominion is getting bolder and bolder . . . and your freighter is no match for a Jem'Hadar attack ship."

"They'd have to catch me first."

"You're really not worried, are you?" He would have thought it impossible, but her smile brightened even further, assumed a fierceness that recalled certain moments they had shared not an hour before.

"Me?" she asked. "I'm fearless. You know that. That's why you love me."

"I think I follow that logic . . ."

His mood, roller-coasting up and down, had just found a new and peaceful equilibrium when something—

For just a moment he thought that he saw Worf, his Klingon friend and strategic operations officer. But no—it was a human of Worf's size and approximate coloration, with some of the same confidence in his stride. Like the momentary glimpse of the earlier man, this man wore clothes that would have been more in place in, say 1950s Earth, in the striped white shirt and pants that Sisko's mind identified quickly as a New York Yankees baseball uniform. He laughed aloud. Of course! There must be some kind of party going on on the holodeck!

The man looked directly at Sisko—

(So much like Worf. Not the face, which was human, another Afro-European blend, but something in the eyes. And something inside Sisko knew this person, knew that his name was . . . *Willie*. But Willie *who?*)

"Hey, Benny," the man said. "See the game last night?"

Willie/Worf continued to walk by. He seemed not to notice Kasidy at all. Stranger still, Kasidy didn't seem to notice him.

"What?" Sisko asked after the retreating, oddly dressed figure.

Willie/Worf walked a few more paces down the hall, and then disappeared into a doorway.

Sisko stared after him, still confused—dumbfounded really—and aware that his heartbeat had sped up, was trip-hammering against his ribcage. What was happening to him? Why was he reacting so strangely to the mere sight of a crewman—

(A crewman? Then which was he? And why does he remind you of Worf?)

—dressed for a costume party?

"Ben?" Kasidy must have called his name three times before he finally heard her, or was able to respond.

"Who was that?" he asked. More than anything else, he felt an irresistible urge to get to the bottom of this. Now.

"Who was who?" she asked.

For an instant he thought that it was a joke, all some kind of prank being played on him. That was it. His crew knew that he was under stress, and had arranged this to get his mind off his troubles. Dax! It must have been, damn the Old Man's sense of humor, why he'd—

But when he looked into Kasidy's eyes, he knew she was telling the truth. She hadn't the slightest idea what he was talking about, and more to the point, he was scaring her. There was something very wrong here.

Disregarding the abruptness of his decision, he ran over to the door through which the ball playing not-Worf had disappeared. Kasidy, behind him, called after him with concern. "Ben . . . ?" she asked. "Where are you going?"

He didn't answer her. He had no attention to offer her at the moment. All of his attention was on the door. He swiftly keyed in the override code on the door panel and it opened to reveal—

The impossible.

CHAPTER
5

No one who had studied history, or loved old American movies or television could have mistaken what lay on the far side of the door.

Sisko immediately recognized the street lamps, soaring up two stories and then curving down like lilies with white bulbs blossoming at their tips. The smell of auto exhaust cloaked the air like a shroud. Wide-grilled automobiles trundling past belching toxins—cars, taxis, even roaring buses carrying passengers by the dozens. Across a wide expanse of concrete street, crowded with vehicles and pedestrians, a neon sign promoting *Coca-Cola* flashed, its blinking dimly visible in the noon light. Above it a sign read *"Planter's Peanuts—a bag a day for more pep!"* and above that posted high atop a six-story office building, a sign read *CHEVROLET*.

Sisko staggered forward, his senses overwhelmed.

The crowd flowed around him like a stream parting for a pebble. Some pedestrians avoided him politely, some wore an expression of disapproval. Stunned, he realized that they were all human, Earth human. American Earth human. Mid 1950s American Earth human. And all of them, everyone he saw was of European descent.

"I don't—" he muttered to himself. He couldn't make the rest of the words come. What was this? All of this? Was it all a part of the game? But what game? Had he stumbled through the back door of a holo-suite? He reached for his padd, but his uniform and equipment were gone. He stared down at himself, and saw that he wore brown pants, a thin leather belt, scuffed leather shoes. No sensory equipment.

His legs weakened and he stumbled a foot forward, his brain temporarily just . . . not working. That was the only way to put it.

There was a sudden blaring sound and Sisko spun, just in time to see a ton of steel grill and rubber tires screeching, weaving trying to avoid hitting him. He had staggered out into the street, completely disoriented, and was trapped between worlds, between identities, between—

Where am I?

and

Who am I?

—just long enough for the juggernaut to bear down on him. Fear jolted through him like an electric shock. He didn't quite jump aside fast enough, *whoofed* with the shock as the bumper clipped him. The breath huffed out of him explosively. He torqued to the side and tumbled down into a heap.

He lay there, numb and tingling, certain that something inside him was irreparably smashed. Dimly, he heard cars beeping, honking. The murmur of voices: "Is he hurt?" "Did you see that?" "He just stepped in front of that car—" "Isn't that just like a—"

And another, loving voice. Kasidy's voice, calling to him as across a great and nameless gulf. "Ben? Are you hurt?"

SHUFFLE

CHAPTER
6

BEN SISKO lay on the cold corridor floor, Kasidy Yates beside him. He heard the thunder of his heart in his chest, heard his own breathing and wondered, for just a moment, if he was insane.

"Ben," she repeated. "Are you all right?"

Shaken, Benjamin Sisko rose to his feet, too unsteady to really ponder her question. This was bad, and getting worse by the moment. "I'm not sure," he said finally. "I'm really not sure at all."

CHAPTER
7

DS9's INFIRMARY was built more for function than comfort, and Benjamin Sisko had never felt that starkness more than at this moment. He lay on the analyzer table, steadying himself and trying to force his way all the remaining distance to consciousness.

Dr. Bashir, DS9's chief physician, was running tests. Kasidy, Joseph, and his son Jake waited nearby.

"He's awake," Kasidy said, relieved. "Ben, are you all right?"

He was still fighting to get his bearings, but the confusion was dissipating like smoke in a slow wind. "I think so."

"Thank God," Joseph said.

His son punched him lightly on the shoulder. "Hey, Dad—you scared us there for a minute."

Frankly, he was still scared. There were too many things that could conceivably go wrong. Oh, this wasn't a barbaric age, medicine had made many massive advances. This was no twentieth century butcher shop. But there were still a vast cornucopia of diseases and ailments before which even the most advanced medicine was helpless.

Doctor Bashir examined him minutely, head to toe, but especially head, using every device and skill at his command. Finally, as doctors have done for a thousand years, he wagged his head soberly, and said, "All right."

Sisko pushed himself up to a seated position. "What happened?" he asked.

"I'm not sure. Reading some unusual synaptic activity," he said. There was more *between* his words than in them. To Sisko, he added, "The neural patterns are similar to those you experienced last year."

Sisko levered himself up to a seated position. "You mean when I was having those . . ." he groped for the right word. "Visions about Bajor?"

Bashir nodded. "That's right."

"Visions?" Joseph asked. "Does this have something to do with those Prophets you're always telling me about?"

"Could be," Sisko said reluctantly.

"Is he having some kind of relapse?" Kasidy asked. "He's not going to need another operation, is he?" The concern and fear in her voice were obvious.

Again, an expression that had probably clouded the face of doctors since Hippocrates. "I don't know yet," he said. To Sisko, he added, "But I'd like you to remain overnight for observation."

To Sisko, the memory of the doorway, of the

collapse, of the strange vision of the street was already beginning to recede. An old and urgent feeling was taking its place. He needed to work. "Are you sure that's necessary?" Serious irritation had crept into his voice.

"Absolutely," Bashir said. "Take a look at these readings." And he handed a padd to Sisko.

Sisko glanced down at it. Even as his eyes began to move he realized that something was happening. What he held in his hands was lighter than a padd and of a different shape. His vision momentarily clouded. When he focused again, he was staring at a magazine with a garish yellow cover. The word GALAXY was printed at the top in huge red letters. The image on the cover was that of an enormous green worm apparently lusting after a buxom blond in a space suit. The caption, lurid as the drawing, read: "Spawned in darkness!"

The words across the top were the most confusing: October, 1953.

Sisko shook his head. It felt as if the world was sinking away under his feet. He squeezed his eyes shut. *Please,* he said. *Please, when I open my eyes again, let this all be over, let me just have my life. I know I've been complaining, I know things have been too complex, but this is insanity, and I am afraid.*

He opened his eyes again and—
SHUFFLE

CHAPTER
8

"You gonna buy that or not?" the news vendor asked.

Benny Russell said "Sure," and searched his pockets for change. He caught a glimpse of himself in the mirror behind the stand, and was momentarily struck by—something.

What was there about his reflection? It was the same reflection that he had seen uncounted millions of times over the course of his thirty years. Taller now, balder now, and (he had to admit) older now. Negro, in a white man's world. He had to admit that as well, but that was a fact that he had lived with every day of his life, and no occasion for surprise. But when he met his own eyes in the mirror, something . . .

Something . . . made him stop. What was it? He wore a neat but slightly rumpled brown suit and a brown cap, and when he looked down he saw the worn

33

pair of loafers he had patched too often in the past months, always promising himself that he would get new ones as soon as the next check came through.

But when he looked at himself in the mirror, for just an instant he had seen . . . someone else. It was the same man, but yet not the same at all. The man he had seen had worn some kind of a dark tunic with an odd, almost military insignia. His eyes, although haunted, had been strong, and piercing. His carriage had been proud, as if he had spent his life walking taller and more confidently than Benny Russell had ever managed. There was a kind of quiet power in that other man. This was a man used to the responsibilities of command. It was just his imagination, he was sure, the same imagination that had gotten him into trouble since his youth, the ability to slip sideways through reality, through a door that no one else could see and to dream about what might be found there.

He had always had that gift, the ability to watch half of a movie and to come up with a dozen ways it might end; to see the end of a movie and to devise a dozen ways it might have begun; and to regale his family with the answers.

Walking home from the movies, taking the subway back into Harlem with his aunt, telling them stories, telling her other adventures of the men and women— mostly white men and women—they had watched on the screen. Making her laugh and say, "Lord, Lord. What are you going to do with that imagination, boy?"

And seeing that laughter, seeing that love in their

eyes had given young Benny Russell his first hint of what he might do with his life, his first clue about how he might make his way in the world. He knew his ambitions were ridiculous. He knew they were absurd.

Hell—that just wasn't an appropriate dream for him to have. He might dream of being a policeman. Or a fireman. Those were jobs that were open to a bright, hardworking Negro boy who kept his nose clean (fireman was a little more difficult than policeman. There were few Negro firemen in New York in the thirties, but he had confidence that by the time he was ready for the job, the job would be ready for him.)

But a writer? And of the kind of stories that filled young Benny Russell's dreams? He dreamed of aliens, and far planets, and machines ... machines that were like cars that could travel on the ground or fly through the air. Machines that might travel under the water.

There was a library at his school, and in it were books by a man named Jules Verne. And Mr. Verne told wonderful stories of ships that traveled beneath the water, and through the air, and through space. Men like Nemo, Robor, and Cavor lived in young Benny Russell's dreams. For years he longed to be like them: to create wonderful inventions, to travel to far places, and to experience miraculous adventures. But everyone told him that that dream, the dream of traveling in such things was far beyond what a colored man might achieve in this world. That might or might not be true. But he could dream.

At last Benny Russell heard that enough to believe

it; but if he couldn't do those things in reality, perhaps he could still write his own stories. And so he wrote his own stories. His teachers criticized him, and his aunt sometimes tore them up for trash; still, he wrote them, even if he had to hide them behind his bed and in his closet.

He made up names for things that already had names, and renamed people and animals, creating in their place strange and exotic concoctions. And that was why, when he thought (through some momentary illusion of light) that he had seen something or someone in the window that looked like him but couldn't have been, a name popped into his mind instantly.

Captain Benjamin Sisko, Benny said to himself, and grinned at the conceit. *His hawklike visage never wavered as he scanned the tasks before him. The fate of the entire space station was in his hands, and never had so many lives rested so easily—*

"Ah, fella," the news vendor repeated. "Are you gonna buy that or not?" Benny handed the man a few coins, and was amused to see his imagination flaring again. He had long since accustomed himself to it, and was amused at its superimposition on reality. He suddenly saw this vendor as a tiny man with flared ears that joined to a swollen, hyperpronounced brow. His mind even leaped in with a name: *Nog. He's a . . . Ferengi. Avaricious but oddly honorable—*

The vendor was making change, and his voice snapped Benny out of his trance. "Personally, I don't see the attraction."

"What? Attraction to what?" Benny stammered.

Those daydreams will get you into trouble one day, Benny. But first, let's hope they make your fortune.

"Attraction to spaceships, flying saucers, men from Mars." He dropped a few coins in Benny's hand.

"What's wrong with men from Mars?" he asked.

"Nothing, except it's all make-believe. Me—I like war stories. Did you see *From Here to Eternity?* Burt Lancaster standing there, in the middle of Pearl Harbor, machine guns blazing, shooting down those Zeros. If it had been flying saucers . . . forget about it."

Benny chuckled. "Well, it takes all kinds."

"Benny—" a voice said behind him.

Benny turned to see who spoke, simultaneously recognizing the speaker as Albert Macklin. Irish, robust, intelligent, Macklin was a former mechanical engineer who now worked at the same magazine that paid Benny's rent. Benny was usually happy to see Macklin, but as he raised his hands in greeting, something wavered in his sight. A familiar sense came over him, that odd fantasy sense, and for just an instant, it wasn't Albert Macklin who stood in front of him but . . . but . . .

O'Brien. Starfleet engineer. Chief of operations at . . . at . . . The rest eluded him, was just beyond reach of his conscious mind. But close, so very close. Somehow he sensed that it was important, and he felt an old excitement building inside him: there was a story in there, somewhere, and it was clawing its way to the surface.

And, he knew, with an old and growing sense of excitement, it was going to be a corker.

"Hello, Albert."

Macklin's pipe hung from his mouth. He was patting down his pockets, searching for a book of matches. "I thought . . . that is if you're on the way to the office . . ."

Benny finished his sentence for him. "We could walk there together?"

"Exactly," Albert said. He patted his pockets again, evidently still searching for the elusive fire stick.

Mercifully, Benny extended Albert a pack of matches.

"Ah," Albert said nonchalantly. "There they are."

And they walked off together, across Times Square. As they did, Benny took a last glimpse behind him at the newsstand.

Nog the "Ferengi." O'Brien the Engineer. And a commanding Negro officer named Benjamin Sisko. What kind of story was his subconscious stewing up?

CHAPTER
9

FROM TIMES SQUARE they strolled together along Seventh Avenue toward 34th Street, and then over to Fifth Avenue, keeping a companionable silence. Benny had never tired of watching the skyscrapers rising, had never wearied of Manhattan's incessant bustle.

It's the future, he would tell himself. *It's my future, too.*

Off Fifth, not too far from the more expensive shops and offices stood the Arthur Trill building, a seven-story monument to the solid brick construction of the twenties. Several of the offices were leased to publishing concerns, all of which timeshared the services of a single Linotronics machine. There was a fashion magazine on the second story, and a trade rag for real estate salesmen on the third. He had heard (from the usual usually reliable sources) that the auto magazine on the ground floor let out their photo room for photo sessions of a more intimate nature, but he had no direct knowledge of this, nor was he ever likely to get it. He supposed it was just the kind of rumors that floated around a building, the kind of idle talk that made the days seem to pass more quickly.

It was the sixth floor that concerned him, because the sixth floor was the brain center of *Incredible Tales of Scientific Wonder,* the third most successful science fiction magazine in the world, and the source of most of his income. The walls of the office were lined with blown-up covers of past issues, including several which had been based on his own stories.

A series of small cubbyhole offices lined the room, with a larger, glass-enclosed office in the back. This last belonged to the magazine's editor.

The walls were covered with drawings and paintings from the magazine, shelves of reference books, photos, and bizarre souvenirs from South America, Germany, and Japan. There were model airplanes, tanks and spaceships, plastic alien critters of every description, movie posters, and a model of the spike-like Trylon tower from the 1939 World's Fair.

In the center of the room sat a round table where the writers generally gathered. Any of them might be found drifting in and out during the month, but on the first of the month was the only time you were guaranteed to find all of them gathered together. This was a special time, and no one wanted to be tardy. Benny had been late for this ritual before, and had lived to regret it.

He still remembered his first visit to the offices of

Incredible Tales, just three years before. He had already sold five yarns to them, and readers had loved them. They were stories set in his own personal universe, filled with bizarre monsters with names like tribbles and Borg, aliens with names like Vulcans and Klingons. His first fifteen stories had all been rejected, the first six summarily, accompanied by printed forms thanking him for his submission. The seventh rejection slip had contained a personalized note scrawled along the bottom: *Good job—not quite what we're looking for, D.P.*

D.P.! That couldn't have been anyone but Douglas Pabst, *Incredible Tales'* legendary editor, a true giant on the level of Campbell or Gold. To get a note, anything other than that damnable little slip of paper, was an electric experience, one which seemed to mark a turning point in Benny's life and career. From then on, there was no stopping him. It felt like he ate, slept and lived at the battered Remington portable typewriter in his living room (his lucky one, the one stenciled with the drawings of the Trylon and the Perisphere from the 1939 World's Fair), banging out story after story after story until finally one of them arrived with a note that said:

> *This isn't bad. I'd like you to take a look at the creatures you call Borg. I think they should make some kind of communication with the heroes, even though they are mostly machine. Have them say something that our heroes can flip back at them pithily later on. How about: "Resistance is Futile"? Give them a voice, and then try us again.*
> *D.P.*

That had been the beginning. After that point, Benny sold everything he wrote. It had taken three more stories for Pabst to invite Benny to drop by the office, and another two months, and another story accepted, before he actually found the nerve to do so.

Walking through the door that first time felt so awkward. There had been the moment, the anticipated moment when the receptionist asked him what he wanted, and he was terribly afraid she would tell him that deliveries were made on the fourth floor, or that the janitorial service never appeared before five o'clock, or any of the other polite, subtle reminders of his station in life.

Or what if Pabst didn't believe he had actually written the stories? Or what if he decided that he didn't want to publish stories written by a Negro? Or what if . . .

What if . . .

And here, there was a part of him that had to laugh. After all, wasn't science fiction the game of "what if"? Wasn't that one of the three primary postulates which motivated the entire field? They were, in order, "what if," "if only," and "if this goes on." These were the lessons that he had learned from the endless stories of star travel, and spaceships, and time warps, and biological experimentation run amok that he had spent every scraped nickel on since he was seventeen years old, since the most important summer of his life, the summer of 1940.

And ultimately, he was able to turn the same tools back on his fear:

What if Douglas Pabst only cares about the quality of a story, not about the color of its writer?

If only you could find one ally, one man in this world willing to take a chance on you, maybe some of those dreams storming between your ears since that summer would have a chance to reach the wider world.

If this goes on, you'll be too afraid to take any chances at all. This is the time to go for it!

So Benny had come to this office, and the secretary had been polite, a bit surprised, but ultimately . . . pleased? Could *that* have been her reaction? Yes, he thought that it was. And Pabst himself had appeared after she disappeared into his office for less than a minute. The expression on his face was one of intense curiosity. Not disrespect. Not confusion. Not disdain or anger.

Curiosity. The man had extended his hand. That had been three years ago, and Benny had never regretted taking it.

At the moment, three people were seated at the table. Julius and Kay Bass were a husband and wife writing team. At the moment, they sat sipping coffee. Julius was a friendly, elegantly attired Englishman who usually wore an ascot. A cigarette holder was clipped delicately between the fingers of his right hand. His wife Kay sat perched on the table. She was a decidedly attractive woman with a no-nonsense attitude and a cutting sense of humor—

Bashir

Kira

There it went *again,* and Benny wasn't certain what was triggering it. His mind was off on another flight of fantasy, and he recognized that whatever engines were roaring down in the creative caverns, they were taking everyone and everything from his environment and adapting them to the task at hand. Bashir/Julius was . . . hmmm. A medical man. Yes, a doctor. Benny could easily see him, using futuristic salves and instruments to save lives. And Kay . . . or Kira . . . she was a security specialist of some kind. Second in command maybe, behind the mysterious (but dashing and handsome) Sisko.

Across the table from them was Herbert Rossoff, a man as opinionated as the day was long, but undeniably brilliant nonetheless. He was the best writer of the group, and he damned well knew it. His attitude sometimes drove Benny slightly nuts, and Benny was delighted by what his imagination devised in vengeance. Rossoff suddenly resembled another "Ferengi," the same bizarre species as the newsboy, his crested brow leading directly into his ears. Hairless pate, and disturbingly sharp teeth. His name was . . .

Quark. Yes, that was it. Egotistical, avaricious, but somehow, in spite of himself, likable.

Kay was busy demonstrating something to her husband. Carefully, she spooned two tablespoons of granulated powder into a glass pitcher of water. She stirred the mixture and the water turned a tannish brown.

"There you go," she said. "A pitcher of plain water instantly becomes a pitcher of ice tea!"

Julius was definitely impressed. "Incredible," he said. "What will they think of next?"

As if hefting a sacred orb, Julius picked up the jar of brown granules and studied the label. "White Rose Redi-Tea," he read. He humphed and then added, "H. G. Wells would approve."

"Hey, Pabst," Herbert called. He had just extracted a doughnut from a box on the table, and taken the first bite. Little flecks of powdered sugar were sprinkled on his chin. "Get out here," his words were muffled by doughnut.

Douglas Pabst appeared, looking a bit weary, as if he had just spent the last thirty-six hours poring over manuscripts, and of course, it was perfectly possible that he had. "What's wrong now, Herb?"

There was something odd about Pabst today—and Benny found his imagination filling in the blank. He had seen the man interact in too many different surroundings: parties, press conferences, talking to illustrators and artists, writers, repairmen, and creditors, and with each of them he took a slightly different tack, as if he had a protean talent for molding himself to the necessary interaction. He saw Pabst as fluid . . . yielding. Suddenly, and rather amusingly, he had an image of Pabst pouring himself into a mold . . . reforming into an editor, and then seeping through the floor.

Benny was almost beside himself with excitement. Unbidden, his muse was absolutely working overtime

45

creating yet another character, another bizarre creature for a story that had yet to even be triggered. That story might not be birthed for months yet, but whatever it was already seemed peopled to the bursting point.

Odo, he thought. The name had just popped into his mind, unbidden, as had the others. *His name is Odo.*

Benny repressed a giggle. He had done this before, had transmogrified real people into fictional characters, but usually only if he was fairly certain they would never read the story. If he did this, if he transformed these people, friends, and associates into characters in a book, he would have to be very careful to keep them from ever guessing what he had done.

"What's wrong now, Herb?" Pabst said wearily.

Herb held up a doughnut. "I'll give you one guess," he said.

Kay wagged her head. "The battle of the doughnuts, round twenty-eight."

Pabst groaned. "That's what you called me out here for—to complain about the doughnuts?"

Herbert mimed biting into a cruller. "They're stale again, Doug."

He thrust the box rather aggressively at Pabst's chest. For a moment it was a standoff, then Pabst took a chocolate glazed pastry from the box and bit down. He chewed, never taking his eyes off Herbert. "Delicious," he announced.

"Delicious my eye," Herbert said pugnaciously. "These are two days old and you know it."

"I've been eating doughnuts my whole life, and

these weren't baked more than—," he took another bite, and this time used the exaggerated delicacy of a seasoned wine taster, "—six hours ago."

It was a lie, and they all knew it was a lie. Everyone in the office knew that if they were to go to the corner bakery today, and see what confections remained unsold by closing time, those same doughnuts would appear in the *Incredible Tales* office come tomorrow. Or the next day.

He glanced around the room, finally seeming to notice Benny. "Here. Apparently, we have a labor dispute. Yours may be the deciding vote." Benny chose a disk filled with red jelly, reasoning that the moist filling would keep the doughnut tasty longer. He bit into it, and found it fine. A little hard, but perfectly edible. Hell, he was used to day-old bread. No problem.

"Fine," he said.

"What's the world coming to?" Herbert said. "Labor siding with management. He threw up his hands. "That's it. I quit. I'm going over to *Galaxy.*"

Pabst sneered. "That rag?"

"I bet that rag knows the difference between a doughnut and a doorstop."

"You want to go to *Galaxy,* go ahead. But they're not going to pay you four cents a word for your stories."

Benny looked to Kay and Julius. "Who's winning?" he asked.

Kay's smile would have done credit to the Mona Lisa. "A draw. Same as always."

Julius, on the other hand, was suddenly quite

47

interested in the discussion. "You're paying him four cents a word?"

"Stay out of this, Julius," Pabst warned. There was no room for equivocation when he used that tone.

Albert might have been prepared to offer a comment, but suddenly found himself quite interested in his missing matches again. He patted his pockets. "Did you . . . ah . . . see where I put. . . ?"

Benny was glad for the chance to deal himself out of the discussion. "The matches? I gave them to you."

Albert kept patting himself, without result. "Then they should be here . . ."

Julius wasn't ready to let it go. "If he's getting four," Julius insisted, "Kay and I should at least get three."

Herbert seemed almost sadistically happy to pounce. "For that fantasy crap you write? You're lucky to be getting two."

Julius colored. "I beg your pardon?"

Kay leaped in, stabbed a finger at Benny's magazine like a matron on the *Titanic* might have pointed out a life preserver. "What's that?"

Benny extracted it from his side pocket. "The latest *Galaxy.*"

She plucked it from Benny's hands. "Hey. Benny has the new *Galaxy!*"

And *that* finally got everyone's attention. Herbert snatched the magazine from Kay.

"Hmmm," he said, eyes scanning swiftly. "Heinlein, Bova, Smith . . . quite a lineup. Add Herbert Rossoff and it's complete!"

Pabst sighed. "What if I promised you fresh dough-nuts tomorrow?"

"Why should I believe you?"

"I'll even throw in a couple of cream puffs."

At that, Rossoff's eyes began to gleam. "Okay . . . I'll stay."

Julius snorted. "Don't do us any favors."

Pabst held up his hands, trying to signal an end to hostilities. "All right, now that we've taken care of the old business—," he pitched his half-eaten doughnut into the trash can, where it thudded with a resounding clunk, "—on to the new. Time to hand out next month's story assignments!" His voice raised to a booming pitch. "Ritterhouse!" he called. "We're waiting!"

From the back of the offices came an answering call. "Coming!" A moment later Roy Ritterhouse emerged, carrying a folder of pencil sketches. Roy was a powerhouse, burly, but always cheerful, a man who truly enjoyed his work. Benny liked him.

But at the moment, staring at him, he saw someone else. Someone with the deeply furrowed brow, dusky skin and attached ears of that Klingon race from his earlier stories. And his name was . . .

Martok.

"All right, friends, and neighbors," the big man said. "Let's see what Uncle Roy brought you today!"

He held up the first sketch proudly. It was a drawing of a little girl standing in the woods near a picnic table. Her gaze was riveted on two aliens in space suits.

Pabst craned his neck at it. "I've titled this one 'Please, Take Me With You.'" He seemed very proud of himself. "Who wants this one?"

This was the Game, and it was one which Benny had taken to like a fish to water. On the first day of the month, Pabst invited a select group of his very favorite writers into the office to witness the unveiling of Roy's month-long labors. Some paintings were wonderful. Some were dreadful. Most were on some slippery slope in between. The trick was to *never* speak up if you weren't sure, absolutely, positively sure that you could do something good with the picture, and that it genuinely sparked your imagination. If you spoke too soon and staked your claim to one of the early paintings, you might miss out on something even better later on. Worst, you might get it home and find out that you didn't really have a decent idea to go with the image, and end up slogging your way through some 12,000 word morass which Pabst would choke on.

Two, maybe three real duds, and you were no longer a member of that select group. That had happened more than once, to both aspiring newcomers and a couple of seasoned pros who had simply bitten off worse than they could chew.

Of course, on the other hand, you could wait too long and end up with some gawdawful image that Pabst, for his own perverse reasons, had fallen completely in love with. There were only so many giant sex-crazed Martian worm stories one could write before needing a long vacation in the rubber room.

Julius seemed to have gotten the go-ahead from his wife. "I think we can do something like that," he said.

Rossoff's smile was battery acid. "What a surprise," he sneered. "I can see it now—the lonely little girl, befriended by empathetic aliens who teach her how to smile." He shuddered as if the thought roiled his stomach worse than Pabst's doughnuts. "It's enough to make you go out and buy a television."

Julius smiled politely, and Benny had a sudden hunch that he wasn't the only one who occasionally placed actual people in his stories. And for all of Julius' apparent placidity, he could, sometimes, dispose of certain characters quite gruesomely, and Benny wondered how many of them were secretly named Herbert Rossoff.

Roy held up another drawing. This one had a bug-eyed monster climbing over the ledge of an apartment building, about to crawl onto the rooftop where a buxom lady sunbathed on a towel.

Kay winced. "You have got to be kidding, Roy."

The big man shrugged. "What can I say? I must've had too much sauerkraut on my hot dogs that night— it gave me bad dreams."

Herbert sputtered, trapped between art and avarice. "That's the worst piece of crap I've ever seen," he began, and then sighed. "I'll take it."

"Of course you will," Julius said gleefully. "You've an affinity for trash, don't you?"

Herbert held the drawing, turning it this way and that, as if framing it in his mind. "The picture may be trash," he said, and his voice was already beginning to take on a dreamy tone that Benny recognized easily. "But once I'm done with the story, the story will be art."

Julius smiled thinly, and quoted his favorite limerick:

> There once was a painter named Seff
> Who was color-blind, palsied and deaf.
> When he asked to be touted,
> The critics all shouted:
> 'This is Art—with a capital F.'

Herbert smiled thinly and said two words: "Four cents."

Benny began to rummage through the remainder of Roy's illustrations. They were a nice bunch, actually, much better than those produced on the not infrequent occasions when the big man fought with his chubby wife, drank, and slept on the sofa. On those occasions, he produced nightmares that looked like they had crawled out of that kid Ellison's mind.

This time, there were creatures of varying shapes and sizes, odd astronomical anomalies, and weather formations never seen by man or framed by God. Albert rummaged with him, going *oooh!* with that one, or *aah!* for the other, but never quite aligning with any of them . . .

Until one of them caught Albert's attention. It was a drawing of a space station. It looked rather like a flat disk bisecting a pair of parentheses. A spaceship or something was docking with the tip. Benny stared at it, and his heart began to beat a little faster.

Benny hardly knew when Pabst came up behind him. "I don't have a title for it yet," Pabst apologized.

"That's all right," Benny said, the dream rising up more strongly now. "I'll think of something."

Benny continued to stare at the illustration. In his mind, the station began to revolve. He imagined that he saw the ships sliding, coasting on energy sails against an ocean of night, their ports the stars themselves. He thought he could almost see tiny faces in the windows of the space station, for that was almost certainly what it was. It was a station, and it was a work of practiced men. This wasn't the first such that they had built. How many before her? Five? Ten?

Somehow, nine seemed the right number.

Pabst's voice broke him out of his reverie. "By the way," Pabst said. "Some of our readers have been writing in, wanting to know what you people look like."

"Write back and tell them we look like writers," Kay said. "Poor, needy, and incredibly attractive." She snorted, but somehow managed to make it an attractive, quite ladylike snort.

Pabst continued. "The publisher has come up with a better idea. Mister Stone has decided to run a picture of you in next month's issue."

Albert rolled his eyes. "Is this absolutely . . ."

"Necessary?" Pabst asked. "I'm afraid so." But now his face darkened a bit and he looked a little embarrassed. "Kay?" he said hesitantly. "You can sleep late that day."

There was a long beat. When she spoke, her expression and voice were atypically acid. "Of course I can.

God forbid the public ever found out K.C. Hunter is a woman."

Pabst smiled sickly. It was clear to Benny that he didn't enjoy what he had just done. It was even clearer that everyone in the office understood that Pabst's next task was inevitable.

He was an employer, but Benny had dared to consider him a friend. And he would not have his friend have to give such news, make such a request as the one which had to follow. "I suppose I'm sleeping late that day, too," Benny said. And hoped that he had kept the bitterness from his voice.

"It's not personal, Benny," Pabst said quietly. "But as far as our readers are concerned, Benny Russell is as white as they are. Let's just leave it that way."

There was silence in the office for a long, embarrassed moment, a silence broken only by the distant sound of automobile horns on the street below. Benny shifted his glance to the floor, and then out of the window. Distantly, the Empire State building rose above the skyline, pointing to the stars.

Herbert was the first to speak. Of course. "Well. If the world's not ready for a woman writer—imagine what would happen if it learned about a Negro with a typewriter—run for the hills! Its the end of civilization!"

Benny took a deep breath, and was almost shocked to hear himself speak, knew that if he didn't get his words out swiftly, he wouldn't be able to speak them at all. "What about James Baldwin," he asked plaintively. "Richard Wright? Ever heard of Zora Neale Hurston, Langston Hughes?"

Pabst was dismissive, but not unkind, and behind his words was a damnably implacable *reasonableness*. "That's literature for liberals and intellectuals," he said, as if he was speaking to children. "The average reader isn't going to spend his hard-earned cash on stories written by Negroes."

Herbert choked back a groan. "Would someone please shoot me and put me out of my misery?"

Julius narrowed his eyes. "How I long for a gun."

Benny closed his eyes, seeking some inner space to maintain, trying to control his temper and maintain his dignity; he felt the effort slipping through his fingers—

But in that darkness, again, everything was different. He wasn't a black man surrounded by whites. He was an Earth man, one of three in the room: O'Brien, Bashir, and the others. They were, in comparison with the aliens, closer than triplets. But even with that genetic and cultural gulf, he and all of those in the room—Dax, Odo, Kira, Bashir and O'Brien—they were all, if not friends, comrades. They had saved each other's lives, bound each other's wounds. In another time, the petty differences meant less than nothing. They were individual aspects to celebrate. But that was another time.

A better time.

He opened his eyes again and was back in the offices of *Incredible Tales*. The silence was oppressive.

"I'm sorry, Benny," Pabst said. "I wish things were different, but they're not."

"Wishing never changed a damn thing," Benny said bitterly.

"Come on, Benny. It's just a photo."

Benny looked Pabst in the eyes, and as he did he heard his mother's voice, saying: *"When I was a girl we couldn't look no white folks dead in their eyes. That made them think that you thought you were as good as them. They don't like that. Little black boys who acted like that used to get lynched. So you be careful . . ."*

But Benny had fought a war to defend his country. He had seen white boys who were just as scared as he could ever have been. Who, under fire, behaved just as stupidly as any coon butler in a bad comedy. And he knew that they were no better. He knew it. He knew it.

Even if he couldn't prove it.

He thought of many things that he wanted to say. He wanted to scream out the unfairness of it, but ultimately all he could say was: "I'll try to remember that."

Pabst looked around for support, but the others were frozen in solidarity for once, for all of their bickering, all of them knew that this was pure bull. They were all respectful of each other's minds and words. The offices of *Incredible Tales* formed a kind of sanctuary, a fortress against the mundane world which their imaginations had rejected and embellished. Now, suddenly, into their private little protective aerie had crept a bit of real-world ugliness, and it stole some of the magic from their lives.

True, Kay couldn't get *her* picture in, either. But that didn't stop her from living in any neighborhood where she could afford a house. It didn't stop her children from attending the best schools, or being served in the finest restaurants, or healed in the best hospitals. What was a matter of ego for Kay was survival for Benny.

And it was almost as if he was on an ice floe, suddenly separated from the rest of them, drifting in a current that was old before any of them were born. They hated that. In that moment, they were ashamed of the privilege they had been born to, and sought some means of expressing their disapproval of something that none of them could change.

And despite the fact that they were writers—fine writers—the clever words eluded them. There was no witty repartee, no logical argument, no appeal to some higher American ideal. The only thing to pierce that oppressive silence was Herbert Rossoff's mutter: "You're a dog, Pabst."

Benny could barely breathe. He felt so ashamed that he wanted to flee from the office, to hide. Who was he to think that he could find haven here, could find acceptance for his mind and his heart among these strangers. Better that he had stayed uptown, even with its memories—

"All right, enough jawing," Pabst said. Apparently, he had decided that there was no graceful way out of this. "Enough standing around. Get back to work."

And with that, he headed back into his office.

Benny glanced at the others, and then, almost accidentally, his eye fell on the glittering model of the Trylon tower. He felt as if he were about to fall over. He had to get out of there, but there was something about the tower. Something about the fair, something that pried up the edge of his memory and tugged at him, something he couldn't quite conjure out of the dark.

Something from the summer of 1940.

Benny stumbled out of the office, clutching the picture to his chest, and made it to the stairwell. He couldn't handle the elevator—not today. Its confined spaces would have suffocated him. He needed room.

He managed to make it halfway down the stairs before he stopped, in shadow, leaning against the wall and sobbing for breath. What had just happened had been beyond humiliating. It had been a basic denial of his humanity. Why did he subject himself to this crap? Why? What was it that drove him, that pushed him to scratch black ink on white paper, to take his private dreams and offer them up to a world that cared not a damn for the dreamer?

Why couldn't he just walk away from it all? He had asked himself that question a thousand times, and had no answer.

Except . . .

The Trylon . . .

SHUFFLE

CHAPTER
10

July, 1940

SUMMER IN HARLEM, 1940, was an oasis of calm for Benny Russell. He was sixteen, a high school senior next year—assuming that he could make up the classes lost through a bout with pneumonia. He was lucky at that; two years earlier, the same disease had cost his mother her life.

But he was young, and alive, and filled with hope, and knew that this might be the last time that he would ever feel totally secure in the world he had known since childhood.

He had grown up amidst the tenements and stoops of 127th and Park—knew every alley, every shadow; he had played basketball in the corner lots; and he knew the cops and the guys down at the youth center by sight and by voice.

His gangly body was too light for football, too slow for basketball. His eyes not good enough for baseball.

And as for boxing, well, let's just say that he liked his nose right where it was, thank you. It might have been nice to be the neighborhood sports hero, but that job was already claimed, and the claimant's name was Willie Hawkins.

Willie was the best athlete in the borough, and everyone knew that. Running, boxing, basketball, football—you just didn't mess with, or bet against Willie Hawkins. He seemed to have always been taller, and stronger, and just *better* than any of the other kids. If there was any problem with that excellence, it lay in the fact that Willie Hawkins was totally aware of his superiority. You could see it in his stride, in his strut, in the way he told jokes with the confident knowledge that the real joke had been played on everyone but Willie Hawkins.

Worst of all, the girls knew it.

In general, Benny didn't care about what girls thought of Willie Hawkins. From the time Willie was in eighth grade, grown women had paid call on the lanky, muscular teenager, had picked him up in their cars, had stopped him on the street to engage him in conversation. That was merely the legend of Willie Hawkins, and that was just the way the world worked.

There was on only one place that it hurt, only one place where he wished that he could match Willie. That was on the occasions that he saw Jenny watching him.

Benny stood watching Jenny approach him now, that familiar sway in her walk. She was beautiful, tall, slender. Maybe she wore too much makeup, laughed too loud, stayed up too late. Maybe the older boys whispered about her after she walked past, and maybe she had been seen getting into too many of their cars. But she was still the most beautiful thing in Harlem, and she belonged to Willie Hawkins, whenever he wanted her.

One day, (Benny was certain), he would tell Jenny what he thought of her. He would tell her that she was a princess, and that no one could understand or appreciate her but him. Until that day, until he found the courage for that confrontation, he would have to hold his tongue, and simply deal with the pain whenever he saw her with Willie and his crowd.

Today, however, he didn't have to. This was a very special day, and he would have a chance to spend it with Jenny, and Willie wouldn't have much to say about it at all.

But she had barely reached Benny and offered her greeting when a chopped Chevy filled with laughing, brown-skinned boys pulled up next to the stoop.

"Hey, Jenny," Willie called, his too-white teeth gleaming. "Why don't you forget about the fair, come on down and watch me hit the ball." He paused. "Promise I'll hit one out of the park for you."

"Maybe tomorrow," she laughed back. "Unk's been promising me this all year."

Willie smirked. He could have almost any girl that he wanted—and dangled them on strings. But he seemed to take special pleasure in his ownership of Jenny. He would ignore her until she began to openly date other boys, and then reel her back in like a fisherman with a trout. He had begun the game back in fifth grade, and had yet to tire of it.

Not that Benny could blame her. He saw the way she looked at Willie. The way everyone looked at him. When they played basketball at school, and went shirts and skins, and they bumped against each other, slicked with sweat and grunting with exertion, showing off their moves, their young, immortal, muscled bodies, Willie was far above all of them, almost godlike in his physical perfection, coordination, sheer animal magnetism.

Hell, who could blame her?

Hell, if he was a woman, *he* would want Willie, not a skinny little spit like Benny. A future professional champ, not a broke-ass little orphan living with his number-running aunt.

There wasn't even any competition, really. And yet . . .

"Hey Benny!" Willie called out.

"Yeah?"

"Take care of my best girl!"

Benny just nodded dumbly as Willie whooped and slapped the side of the Chevy. The car belched smoke and roared off down the street.

Jenny paused at the stoop, and smiled up at Benny. Her smile filled the whole world. "Well," she said. "This is a day! 'Bojangles!' " she said.

"Bojangles!" Benny replied. He mimed a little dance step. "You ready to go see the best damned dancer in the whole world?"

"I can't wait," she said.

She may have been Willie's girlfriend, but today,

just today, Benny could pretend that she was his. Today, they were going across to Flushing Meadow, to the World's Fair, to see the legendary Bill "Bojangles" Robinson dance. As they began to walk down the street toward the youth center, he could imagine that she linked her arm through his arm, imagine that she was going out with him, not just for a day at the World's Fair, one arranged by the Youth Center during the fair's Negro Week.

At the fair, they would treat themselves to exhibits extolling the contributions of Negro Americans to the greatness that was America. It was a thing to inspire pride, and inspiration was something to cherish in this day and age.

But he knew that when the day was over, he would return her to Willie: he remembered Hawkins' "take care of my best girl" comment, and knew that it was true. This was a loan, a very *temporary* loan.

But for the next few hours, he was going to pretend that it wasn't. He would pretend that this summer day, with its cheery sun and promise of adventure to come, was just another in an endless stretch of days that the two had enjoyed together. He would pretend, in effect, that this town was his oyster, and that the girl beside him was his. And just maybe if he dreamed hard enough, it would one day be true.

The Park Avenue youth center was a central meeting place for the young kids between the ages of nineteen and about eleven. There was always something happening, always a sense of activity, always a bustle.

When they entered it was, at the moment, filled with the busy sound of a dozen bodies—scuffing leather in the boxing ring, and in the lot just outside, bouncing around the basketball court at a dizzying pace.

For a minute, he thought that his eyes deceived him, that a kid of nine or so was out on that court, but when he had the chance to watch from another angle, he saw that it was little Cassie out there. Cassie was a tomboy to the limit, the kind that it was difficult to imagine ever putting on a dress. She was only a year younger than he was, but—embarrassingly—she had all of the athletic prowess that he had been denied.

More embarrassingly, she had an irritating tendency to want to tag along with him. Perhaps she wouldn't spot him today, and he could just slip past—

No such luck. "Benny!" she called out, her dark, oval face suffused with pleasure. "Sorry," she said to the boys on the court.

Jenny laughed musically, and her smile was pure tolerance. "It looks like your fan club spotted you," she grinned.

"Aww . . . I don't know why she does that," he said.

Jenny wagged her head. "No, you really don't, do you?" she asked, and laughed. "Hi, Cassie."

Cassie glared at Jenny, but she had to tilt her head up to do it. Jenny had the height as well as the natural charm and grace, all of the things that Cassie lacked. He suspected that in a few years, Cassie might be spectacularly beautiful, but right now, he just wished that she would leave him alone. It was embarrassing to have her follow him around, and he wished that she would just go and bug someone else.

Her dark face was dotted with perspiration, and she was breathing hard. "Are you ready?" she panted. Then almost as if she hadn't noticed Jenny was there, turned and looked up at her, smiling mildly. "Oh," she said. "Hi, Jenny."

His heart sank. "You're going to the fair?" he said despondently. His image, his dream of having Jenny all to himself through a long, and ultimately, romantic day was beginning to fray around the edges.

"Heck, yeah," she said. "Mr. Cooley said that anyone who wanted to come today could come, if they had the money."

Cooley was the Youth Center's director. He was also, during the school year, the science teacher at Lenox High, the man who had guided Benny during the past year or so, guiding him steadily, gently but firmly away from trade classes and toward science and English. He was also Jenny's uncle.

"You've got talent, boy," Cooley had said to Benny once. "But you're going to have to work to bring it out."

Talent? That was a word that Benny would never have applied to himself. He had been a quiet, bookish boy through most of his life, the last chosen for any game that required strength or skill. He was certainly no Willie Hawkins, but he knew that he did have a brain. One day, he would run numbers for Big Sid, maybe work his way up into the policy operation. There was money there, and money made the difference in this world.

"Well," he said, trying another tactic. "Why would you want to go on out there anyway? Anyway, where would you get seventy-five cents?"

"My grandma gave it to me," she said, and for a moment he thought she was actually going to stick her tongue out at him. "This being Negro Week and all, she thought I should go and see what it's all about and come back and tell her."

He sighed. It was useless to argue. The fair was only an hour away, but that might as well have been a world for the poorer residents of Harlem. Seventy-five cents just to get in! Then there was transportation and food once on the far side of the gate. That could be prohibitive unless you brought a box lunch, as he and Jenny had.

There was even a certain sense that the fair wasn't for Negroes. It was for the white folks who had built it, that's what it was. But Benny had yearned to go to it since he had first heard about it. There was something about that fair, and the promise of the future that it represented. But that was too high-falootin' to actually motivate him to go, until Mr. Cooley announced that Bill "Bojangles" Robinson (the greatest dancer in the world!) was slated to perform there. That was different. In fact, that made *all* the difference.

Suddenly, his aunt managed to find the seventy-five cents for him. And suddenly, it was permissible for him to fantasize about the other delights he might find there.

The days of his life might well be filled with deprivation. Maybe the walls of his tenement were thin enough to hear the neighbors snoring or fighting or making love. Maybe there were so few jobs in the neighborhood that his father had been forced to travel further and further every day to find a decent wage, until he was leaving for weeks at a time, and then months, trying to find a place to play his piano. Then five years ago, he had simply not come home at all.

Maybe there was so little hope to be had that his aunt was absolutely addicted to the numbers, that gambling fever derisively called "nigger stocks," a way for the poor to vicariously experience the thrill of the stock market. Every day, the closing numbers of the New York Stock Exchange were published in the *Times*. Every day his aunt, and countless thousands like her, had the chance to bet a penny or a nickel or a dollar on a three-digit number, and take the chance on earning six dollars for every penny they invested if that number matched the last three published in the next day's paper.

He had tried to tell her that this didn't make any sense, that she would invest a thousand pennies for every six-dollar win, but she was convinced that that weekly dollar would pay off one day, and that she would use that money to pay off the bills that choked her, stop collecting numbers slips for Big Sid and maybe even move to New Jersey, where she had a sister who was working for the county, and could get her a job.

First, she had to get ahead of the bills, because otherwise she wouldn't be able to move.

Hope was a business, and his aunt Ardelia had invested heavily therein.

Mr. Cooley rapped on the front door, smiling at them. He was a tall drink of water, with a protruding Adam's apple and a pair of thick glasses, which made him look like a goldfish peering through the side of its bowl.

"Well," he called, "I guess everyone's here!" Another dozen kids appeared from around the gym: all had been playing ball, or reading, or listening to the radio from which Benny Goodman's swing played exuberantly. (For a white boy, Goodman could really jam, and Benny wasn't too embarrassed by the similarity of names.)

As a group, the dozen or so of them trooped down the block to the subway station, passing a burned-out tenement as they did. Benny remembered hearing the firetrucks a week before, a distant keening in the night. People were without homes now. Maybe someone had died. He remembered his mother telling him about a fire she had seen as a girl, people trapped on the upper floors, jumping to their deaths even before the fire reached them. He swore that he would get his mother out of here one day.

Her death had ended *that* dream. Maybe . . . just maybe he could do it for Ardelia. He didn't want her to have to live like this.

And God knew, he wouldn't want to die like *that*.

At the subway station, they paid their money to ride downtown. The train was pretty empty at this time of the morning and all of the faces on it were dark.

As they got closer and closer to downtown, more

and more white faces piled on. Ordinarily, he knew that Caucasians looked at him, and people like him with a certain fear and distrust, a sense that there was something wrong with the world because they were forced to share their precious breathing space with Negroes. But today, and for the past year, it had been just a little different. Today they were all adventurers heading in the same direction. Today they were all fairgoers, gone to take just a peek at the future, the world in which all of them would live. That made a difference.

"Listen to the fight last night, Benny?" Cassie said, looking up at him. A love of boxing was one of the few things that he had to admit they had in common. "Armstrong almost killed that bum!"

Cassie went into a little of a boxer's crouch, and mimed a couple of punches. Pow! She was Henry Armstrong, Welterweight Champ of the world. Bang! She was Joe Louis, greatest boxer who ever lived.

"Yeah, I listened."

Cassie aimed her last punch at his chin, and Benny pretended to wobble as the car began to roll. "I'm telling you," she said. "One of these days there's going to be women's boxing, you know, and I think that I could do real good." She looked up at Jenny. "What do you think?"

"I think," Jenny said. "That in a couple of years, you're going to forget about all of this stuff, and find out that you're a girl. That's what I think."

Benny choked back a laugh. He tried to imagine Cassie in anything other than her trademarked sneakers and pants, and couldn't, quite. Cassie looked at Jenny with her mouth flattened into a thin line. "Not me," she said. "I'm going straight for the top."

Benny loved her at that moment. Like a sister, of course, but he loved her. Unlike most of the people that he knew, or had ever known, Cassie could dream.

Benny worked his way up next to Cooley, who had a faraway look in his eye. "You thinking about Bojangles?"

Cooley shook his head "no."

"Still thinking about that Futurama thing?"

Cooley shook his head, and his eyes seemed to gleam, set in his face like a pair of dark pearls. "No, there's a special exhibition this week," he said.

"What's that?" Benny asked.

"Well, you know that this is Negro Week at the fair, so it had solicited some additional participation from African nations," he said.

"And what did they get?" Benny asked.

A heavyset Negro man, his face a succession of dark heavy folds, had listened to the conversation with growing amusement. "Africa?" the heavy man said. "They ain't got nothing to send over but maybe a crate of monkeys and bananas," he said. "I been out to that damn fair—ain't nothing out there but white people. Don't get your little heart up."

"That's not really true," Cooley said. "The *Harp* sculpture is actually the work of a Negro, Augusta Savage. And the *Democracity* song is the work of a Negro, as well."

The worker's thick mouth twisted into a sneer. "You talk real smart, but you ain't doing these kids no favor. They're just niggers, and that's all they're ever gonna be."

Their car pulled into the station and Cooley shepherded them off eagerly, happy to get them away from the inebriate. And Benny was happy to go.

He looked back, feeling sad, and angry, and maybe just a little fearful. What right did this drunk have to spoil his day? It was an adventure, and that was all that there was to it. It was going to be a *great* adventure, one that he would remember his whole life. That he was sure of.

They changed trains downtown at Penn Station. Penn was a magnificent granite and marble building two city blocks long. Benny had never been there before, and his mouth dropped open at the sheer scale of the station: the mere pedestals on which the columns stood were taller than Benny. The concourse looked like something from a fantasy, a staggering open space crisscrossed with steel and glass, a ceiling so high it seemed there should have been clouds beneath it.

Benny stared, stupefied, as Cooley led them toward their train.

He hadn't even gotten to the Fair, and his brain was already buzzing! Benny worked his way over close to Cooley again, and asked him, "So what is this special exhibit?"

Cooley mopped his forehead, as if the afternoon sun had already begun to beat on them all. "You'll just have to wait and see," he said. "It's in the Hall of Nations, though." It was clear that the old black man's tirade had jarred Cooley, and it was taking him a little while to get his emotions back under control.

"The Hall of Nations?" Jenny asked.

"Yes. Most countries have their own exhibition space, but the Fair has areas set aside for some of the smaller, or poorer nations, and there are a couple of African exhibits that are supposed to be . . ." he paused, "quite interesting. Really quite." He leaned back against one of the support posts with a small, mysterious smile on his face. He seemed to have regained his equilibrium. "Yes," he said, "quite."

The train ride from midtown Manhattan was only ten minutes along the Long Island Rail Road. The special train emptied them out into the station to join a throng, a veritable sea of people heading down and across the promenade toward the gates of the fair. Even though Benny had tried to maintain a cool demeanor, the sight of the Trylon and the Perisphere made his heart race and trip-hammer in a way reminiscent of how he felt when he looked at Jenny.

(Or the way Cassie feels when she looks at you, Benny?)

He looked down at the friend at his side, and she looked so happy and carefree, so happy just to be here, and alive, to be a part of this crowd entering the fairgrounds, that he didn't really want to answer, or have an answer to that question. Not just now. Right now, what he wanted to do was to appreciate the work, be a part of the crowd, and find his way into the world of tomorrow.

Flushing Meadow, the site of the 1939 World's Fair,

had once been known as the Corona Dumps, a tidal expanse covering 1,216 acres along the Flushing River. For decades it had merely been a refuse dump for the Brooklyn Ash Removal firm. Now, overseen by a nonprofit corporation, funded by over twenty-seven million dollars in bonds, the former dump had been transformed into one of the wonders of the world. The fair opened on April 30, 1939, the 150th anniversary of George Washington's inauguration. Its symbol was the Trylon and Perisphere, a futuristic structure that housed the exhibit "Democracity." There were seven zones: amusement, communications, community interests, food, government, production and distribution, and transportation. Exhibitors included about sixty countries, the League of Nations, thirty-three states and territories (including Puerto Rico), such federal agencies as the Works Progress Administration, and the City of New York.

According to the newspaper, all kinds of new products were being introduced there. Unbreakable glass called "Lucite," a radio with pictures called "television," a kind of whole-room refrigerator called "air conditioning," and more.

But beside the chance to see Bill Robinson, what Benny wanted most was to see Billy Rose's Aquacade, the "Road of Tomorrow" by the Ford Motor Company, maybe check out the diesel engines in the Railroad Building—Benny had an uncle who had worked for the railroad. Just a Pullman Porter, it was true, but a railroad man, nonetheless. There was also "Micky's Surprise Party," a cartoon by Walt Disney. He loved cartoons.

And if the line wasn't too long, he wanted to take a jump off the Life-Savers Parachute Tower, 250 feet of stomach-dropping fun.

His first impression of the Fair was its sheer size. He had never in his life seen anything so huge. The entire thing was so intimidating—the vast crowds, the complex and confusing maze of passages between exhibits, the constant barrage of sights and sounds— that his mind sought some central object to focus on, and found it in the central structures: the Trylon and the Perisphere. The Trylon was a slender three-sided pylon 610 feet tall, 50 feet higher than the Washington Monument. The Perisphere was almost 200 feet across. It looked like nothing less than God's personal ping-pong ball.

They entered through the IRT and BMT subway gate, each of Cooley's dozen charges paying his seventy-five cents, receiving a little map and program book for their precious coins, and walking out onto Bowling Green. To their left was the Town of Tomorrow exhibit and buildings of Contemporary Arts, and along the Avenue of Patriots, the Home Furnishings and Gas exhibits. They gawked as they went, utterly enchanted. There was, everywhere they strolled, the sound of music and laughter, and the aroma of food that made him wish that he had extra money in his pocket and that he didn't need to rely upon the sandwich in the brown paper bag stuffed into his shirt.

But although the exhibits beckoned to them, they didn't stop—Cooley was of one fierce mind. He was going to guide his charges though the crush and shepherd them to the General Motors exhibit, and he was going to accomplish that at whatever cost. Then, later, they would thrill to the artistry of Bill Robinson.

He was almost out of breath by the time the building rose before them.

The General Motors Futurama building was like an unclimbable silver cliff, the only approach through a narrow red cleft in one side. Two serpentine ramps led up to the slit—it was absolutely mobbed, and they waited in a mile-long line on one of the ramps.

The letters on the General Motors building were silver on silver. As they inched further up the gentle slope of the ramp, again and again his eyes were drawn to the towering Trylon, almost as if it were calling to him. The Future! Everywhere he looked, this whole idea of the "Future" almost screamed to him, and a tiny voice deep inside him finally, with undeniable excitement, asked him if he had ever wondered what his part in that future might be.

Everywhere, music filled the air. Musicians were stationed in small groups around the grounds. Popular music, swing music. Wailing clarinets.

Once inside, he was confronted by a series of trolleys, which the crowd and students piled into. The little cars only allowed two people per ride, separated by a little partition. Cassie tried to jostle her way next to Benny, but some god of probability blessed him, and put him in a cart with Jenny.

It was dark in there. Their shoulders pressed close

together, and for just a moment, he felt her lean against him. Once, when their little cart bumped around a curve, her hand stole out and grasped his.

He felt that contact right down to his core, as though a little jolt of electricity was bouncing around in his marrow. Even though it was probably just the excitement of the moment, that she was enjoying the sights and sounds, even though she released his fingers quickly, he was still left with a tingling memory. It warmed him.

A hidden announcer's voice said: "General Motors invites you on a tour of future America. The moving chairs below the map will transport you to the world of the future—to 1960."

The chair had its own piped-in sound track with music and narration. And then he was flying.

For the next few minutes, Benny was transported on an imaginary flight across an America two decades yet to come. A curved map beneath them gave a perfect illusion of flight, and there were frequent changes of scale, to give you the sensation of swooping down closer or riding higher in your cross-country journey.

They saw cities of the future along the way. Skyscrapers were thrusting tall boxes with rounded edges and wraparound glass walls. A suspension bridge hung from one graceful, central tower. A blimp hangar on a round floating platform could be pointed in any direction. In an apple orchard, individual fruit trees blossomed under individual glass jars.

He held his breath, entranced, and wasn't certain that he began to breathe again until the end of the ride, when he was deposited in a mock-up of a typical American street with the narrator's excited advice to keep his: "Eyes to the future!" still ringing in his ears.

Never in his life had he experienced anything like that, and only one thing could conceivably spoil the experience for him: Every last one of the thousands of little human beings shopping, working, playing, worshipping and living in the cities of the future had been white.

Although other fair exhibits were wonderful, they seemed to pale in comparison with the General Motors exhibit. They stopped for lunch, and sat at a cluster of picnic tables, watching the passersby with a happy, relaxed air. Life was good, and whatever came next, he was going to be ready for that, too.

Cooley had disappeared for a few minutes, promising to meet them back here, and hadn't returned yet. Then they saw him, and he looked gravely disappointed.

"What's wrong, Mr. Cooley?" Benny asked.

"I went over to the Hall of Nations," the teacher said. "I wanted to see how the lines were."

"And?"

"There weren't any lines, because the exhibit isn't open."

Benny felt his mouth open and then close again. It wasn't fair. He knew that Mr. Cooley had chosen *this* day specifically, not to see Bojangles' magic feet— that had just been a lure to get the kids to the fair.

And it wasn't just the Futurama, although he had been enthusiastic, and less disappointed than Benny that there had been no dark faces. There was something else. Something about this Hall of Nations . . .

Benny shared Cooley's sense of disappointment. "Not open?"

"They said that the curator had taken ill, and that he was very protective of the exhibit, had traveled all the way from Africa with it, and wouldn't let anyone else near it, so that that section was locked up."

"What is it?" Benny asked, pressing again.

Cooley seemed to be reluctant to talk about it, and then sighed.

"Well, there's a tribe in Africa called the Dogon—"

"Where?" Jenny asked.

"The Mali Republic. They have a legend that is a little difficult to explain."

"What's that?" Benny asked.

"Well, the story is that thousands of years ago, their ancestors were visited by creatures from another star. Apparently, there was some kind of exchange between them, and the aliens were said to have left something behind."

"Something like what?"

"Well . . . it's only been in the exhibition for a couple of days at this point, like I said, the exhibit is new—but in the paper they said that it looked kind of like a crystal hourglass. He won't let anyone look at it more closely, so no one knows quite what to make of it, but I think it's a real cultural artifact."

"You don't believe the stories about spacemen, do you?"

"No, I think that it might represent an unusual glassblowing or gem cutting from an earlier era of African civilization." He sighed. "I just want to see for myself."

He looked out over the crowd, and his face was painted with sheer discouragement. "Well, we can see some of the other exhibits, and maybe come back. We'll have to get the train before eight o'clock, but maybe that can be done. Maybe. Just maybe we can get the full day in."

He slapped Benny's thin back with one broad, flat hand. "We'll give it our best shot, right?"

"Right," Benny said.

SHUFFLE

CHAPTER 11

1953

BENNY RUSSELL emerged from the *Incredible Tales* office building, staring at the drawing in his hands. There was salvation in that sketch. There was hope. If there was pain

so many kinds of pain, remember, Benny?

—in this world, perhaps there could be peace, or even salvation in another. The space station in the picture looked like such a place, a place which might be home, home to him and a safe haven for a thousand races and species, all meeting as equals, judged only by their actions and capacities, not by accidents of birth.

That dream sustained him.

A sudden gust of wind plucked at the paper, and it tweaked out of his hands and tumbled down the street between the feet of the passing pedestrians. Cursing, he chased after it. The damned thing did an elusive pirouette, tumbling and tossing as if it was consciously attempting to elude him.

Like any dream, its flight was irregular, elusive, just beyond his grasp. He fought to narrow his mind down to the chase. This was no time to allow old problems, old fears and insecurities to stop him from pursuing his goal. It was just a sheet of paper, not his career. Just a pencil sketch, not the shattered fragments of his life.

All of his attention was there, on that sheet of paper, and it was shocking and sudden when a black brogan clomped down on it, pinning the sheet of paper to the ground.

Benny stared at it for almost five seconds before he forced himself to look up, past the blue creased pants, past the heavy leather belt and service revolvers, to the police officers staring at him with barely disguised contempt. Two of them. Both men, of course, were Caucasian.

He blinked. For a moment one of them—the one whose name badge read Ryan—*momentarily fluttered, and another man stood in his place. Then it wasn't a man at all. It was a creature with ridged facial skin, and a high wall of muscle from shoulders to neck. And the name of this person was . . . Gul Dukat. They had been enemies. Not Dukat and Benny*

(who was Benny?)

but Dukat and Captain Sisko. Yes. Dukat had once ruled Sisko's world, and Sisko had deposed him, and animosity ran deep. He was a "Cardassian."

The other wore a name badge saying Mulkahey. *And again, he shimmered in Benny's*

(Benny?)

sight, and took on another form. Weyoun, a . . . "Vorta" . . . that was it. A field supervisor for the Vorta, who had once represented the Dominion in another matter involving Benjamin Sisko, commanding officer of Deep Space . . . Nine. Yes. That was it. Deep Space Nine, an outpost between two empires, a frontier outpost, a safe zone almost like Casablanca. And maybe Sisko was rather like Rick, or a combination of Rick and Captain—

Ryan smacked his nightstick into his palm. Hard. He stared at the oncoming Benny, and there was some part of this man that actually *hoped* that something would go wrong, that hoped that there might be . . . an excuse. Yes, there was really no other word for it . . . to employ some of the force that he was legally entitled to use.

Benny braced himself. This situation, these confrontations, were old and familiar to him, and went back to some place deep, deep within him. If he believed in a racial memory, they went back to some time when men like Ryan and Mulkahey had wielded whips, not truncheons. When they dragged reluctant Negroes away in leg irons, not handcuffs.

There was nothing even remotely friendly in their eyes.

"What's all the hurry?" Ryan asked.

Benny pointed to the piece of paper on the ground. In his most controlled voice, he said: "That piece of paper . . . it's mine."

Ryan made no move to lift his shoe from the paper. "Is that so?"

Benny was silent. He had learned, through long experience, that saying the wrong thing could bring greater pain than not saying enough.

"Nice suit," Mulkahey said, eyes hooded. "Where'd you get it?"

Benny forced his breathing to remain calm. "I bought it. Can I have my drawing back?" Unbidden, a thread of irritation had crept into Benny's voice.

Ryan remained motionless. "Hey," he said. "I'd watch that tone of voice if I were you."

Mulkahey prodded his nightstick in Benny's direction. "What are you doing around here, anyway?" The unspoken subtext? *What makes you think you can shuffle out of Harlem without getting a nightstick so far up your ass you look like a licorice popsicle?*

"I work here," Benny said. Red anger crowded the edges of his vision, but there was black, dead black in the center of it. He recognized both color and shade. There was danger here, more than he wanted to admit. He had to walk very carefully.

"What are you?" Ryan asked snidely. "The janitor?"

Benny wanted to scream at them: *No! Dammit. I'm a writer. I'm a good writer, and I've sold more words than either of you apes have read.*

But he said nothing.

"Awfully well-dressed for a janitor," Mulkahey said.

"How do we know the picture's yours?" Ryan chimed in.

Benny struggled to maintain his composure. "It's a drawing of a space station."

"A what?" Mulkahey narrowed his eyes. "Space what? Are you sassing me?"

Benny tried to find the words. "It's a kind of Flash Gordon thing." He bent down to pick up the paper. Ryan's foot was still planted on it and showed little sign of moving. Benny tugged at it ineffectually.

Mulkahey sneered. "Buck Rogers, that kind of stuff? Mighty flighty aren't you, boy? I think I want to take a look at this 'Space Station.'" He glanced at his partner. "Well, get off it."

A reluctant Ryan obliged. Mulkahey looked at the drawing, turning it around, and there was grudging admiration in his eyes. He looked sharply at Benny.

"You see," Benny said. "It doesn't have any value to any one but me."

"You aren't trying to tell me that you drew this, are you?"

The answer was no. Even if the answer was yes, Benny knew that the reply had to be no. Sudden inspiration hit him. "No, sir," he said, hating his mouth for saying it. "I'm just delivering it for the man in the office."

Both men relaxed. Suddenly the world seemed to make sense to them. "Oh—you're a delivery boy."

"Kinda well dressed for a delivery boy," Ryan said, but still handed the drawing back to Benny.

"All right," Mulkahey said. "Beat it. Take your picture and get out of here."

Benny tried to leave, but Ryan stopped him.

"This time, you're getting off with a warning. Next time, you won't be so lucky."

Benny kept his face carefully neutral. But in his mind, he remembered another time, during the war. Remembered an exploding boiler, and a white boy who looked an awful lot like this man, scalded and dying, his red ropy intestines coiling out of him like a bleeding snake, mewling with fear as death crawled up to claim him.

You aren't so very different from that man, Benny thought to himself. *I'd be lying if I didn't say that it was interesting to see how similar we all are on the inside. I'd be lying to say I wouldn't like to see that again, right here, right now.*

"Go on," Mulkahey said. "Move it."

Benny walked on, with as much dignity as he could muster. But he could hear the two cops behind him:

"I tell you, Kevin. This city's going to hell in a hand basket."

"God damned shame . . ."

Yeah, we're all going to hell, Benny thought. *But you first.*

CHAPTER
12

BENNY TOOK the subway uptown. At first the car was mostly filled with white people, but as it passed further and further north, the whites exited through the hissing doors, replaced by darker faces.

And as they did, Benny found himself relaxing, relaxing in a way that he never could downtown. At every stop, there were fewer and fewer white faces, until the last few Caucasian men and women remaining seemed to shrink into themselves.

The Negroes who boarded were mostly working folk, just like the whites were, but as the last few pale faces scrambled to get off at the last stop before Harlem, he saw a look in their eyes that he sometimes saw in his own when he was downtown.

It's no fun, is it? he thought, and realized that his internal voice was not entirely kind. *It's no fun to be surrounded by aliens, is it? You wonder if they hate you. You wonder why they hate you. You know that you've done nothing, but you can feel, can sense the* otherness *around you, and it pulls you into yourself, doesn't it?*

And as the train rocketed along its tracks, he wondered to himself if the others in the office had any idea what his secret was, any idea what it was that made his work special and made it, in fact, second only to Herbert's in reader popularity.

I know the alien mind. I've been an alien my whole life. Oh, every human being feels that they don't belong. But not every man can get beaten or lynched just for looking another man in the face.

I've been an alien my whole life. Around my own people, brown people, they wondered why I had the dreams I had. They wondered why I liked all types of music. Why I could look at white heroes in movies and cheer for them. Why I could love Rocky Marciano as much as I did Joe Louis. And I couldn't tell them. I don't know myself, even though I know it has something to do with that summer in 1940.

But any white man might be able to say he feels alienated. But take that same white man and plunk him into the middle of Harlem. Make it so that everything that he could ever dream of, aspire to, hope for, belongs to the ones who don't look like him.

Worse yet. Take that white man to a church where the Jesus he prays to is black. Make him spend money with black men's faces on the dollars. Make him listen to speeches by the men who run the country—and let all of them be black. Show him endless pictures of the beautiful people, the ones who hold the American

Dream—and all of those smiling men and women and happy children are black. Give him history books where every hero he is supposed to model himself after, every president who led his country, every philosopher who ever uttered a word worth remembering, every inventor who pushed back the night for the human race was black.

Do all of these things before you tell me that you understand what it is to be the outsider.

I can write aliens because I understand them. More, I can write aliens because I long for a world where we are all alien. In such a world, none of us are alien. We are just all living things, afraid of death and loneliness. And maybe, just maybe, in order to alleviate that fear we will reach out to each other, and find the human heart within the alien breast.

If we are all *aliens, then none of us are.*

The last white face left the subway car, and as it did, the entire car seemed to breathe a sigh of relief, seemed to settle into another rhythm. He felt the tension leave his body, no longer held himself in the slight rigidity which kept his natural physical ease in check, the long, rhythmic stride that seemed to anger white men and intimidate (or intrigue) white women so effortlessly.

He was home.

Yeah, Benny. Home. But how many Negroes, "your own people," understand your dreams? If you are honest with yourself, don't you feel more at home with Kay and Herbert, even Pabst? You have no home, except the inside of your head.

So thank God there is room enough in there for you, and all of your friends, real and imagined, because otherwise it would be a lonely existence indeed.

The car came to a halt, and Benny was at his stop. He passed out of the doors and hopped up the stairs. He always felt about ten pounds lighter in Harlem than he did downtown, as if a great and secret weight had been lifted from his shoulders.

Harlem is a neighborhood in Manhattan, bounded to the north by the Harlem River, to the east by Fifth Avenue, to the south by 110th Street, and to the west by Morningside and St. Nicholas avenues. Its neighborhoods are called Bradhurst, Striver's Row, Manhattanville, Hamilton Heights, and Sugar Hill.

Originally settled by Dutch farmers who named it *Nieuw Haarlem,* it had a checkered history: At Harlem Heights in 1776 the Continental Army defeated British troops advancing to the city. During the 1840s and 1850s many farms were deserted and taken over by Irish squatters.

During the 1880s elevated railroads were extended along Second, Third, Eighth, and Ninth avenues, tenements were built in East Harlem, apartment buildings of the Upper West Side. As the population rose the neighborhood became predominantly German. Attractive "new law" tenements and spacious apartment buildings with elevators were erected between 1898 and 1904, when subway lines were extended along Lenox Avenue.

About this time Negroes first moved to the neighborhood, where they found better housing, a more attractive environment, less racism and violence than in other parts of the city. Most settled near 135th Street.

The neighborhood started falling apart during the First World War—by 1920 most Jews were moving to newer neighborhoods in the West Side and in the Bronx, Brooklyn, and Queens. Between 1920 and 1930 the Negro population of Harlem skyrocketed to over 200,000, while white faces became as rare as an honest politician. Blacks from throughout the nation were soon attracted to the area by economic opportunities and a flourishing cultural life.

Benny still remembered stories of those days, old timers talking about Langston Hughes, Countee Cullen, Zora Neale Hurston, and other writers holding readings and throwing parties that even the rich white folks came uptown to attend.

There were art showings by Romare Bearden, William H. Johnson, and Richmond Barthe; comedy and jazz at theaters on every corner of every neighborhood. Oh, things were swinging then. The names: Jackie "Moms" Mabley, Pigmeat Markham, James P. Johnson, Fats Waller and Willie "the Lion" Smith (oh, that Harlem Stride!), Fletcher Henderson, Duke Ellington, Chick Webb.

The legends: Louis Armstrong and Bessie Smith on the same stage at the Apollo. Coleman Hawkins tearin' it down across the street from the theater where Ethel Waters blew the ceiling to kingdom come.

The Cotton Club, Connie's Inn, Small's Paradise, and the Savoy Ballroom. And the Bebop days, just after the Second War, when giants like Charlie Parker,

Dizzie Gillespie, and Thelonious Monk reigned supreme.

Benny had read the *Amsterdam News* and the *New York Age*, the biggest Negro publications in the country. He heard impassioned civil rights speeches by A. Philip Randolph and W.E.B. Du Bois, and remembered his aunt talking about the one who started it all—Marcus Garvey, the Jamaican immigrant who started America's first Back-to-Africa movement.

But Harlem would be no cornerstone for black progress: the Depression devastated it. Negroes continued to settle in Harlem although work was scarce, and because the rents remained high, apartments were subdivided into ever smaller units; at one point the population density in Harlem was more than twice that of New York as a whole. Harlem was a shadow of its former self, but it was still the world that Benny Russell knew best.

It was almost nine o'clock at night, and there were only a few pedestrians on the street. He knew some, and nodded acknowledgments to some of them, a murmured "Hey, Delroy" or "Gloria—how are the kids?" as he passed among them, heading toward his apartment.

It was strange the way one part of him seemed to go to sleep, and another part awaken when he was here. Different music played from the radios, and the entire world seemed to move to an eccentric rhythm. And it was something that called out to him, exerting a pull as powerful as the stars in Benny's imagination. These streets were his past and present. The stars, his future.

Yes, he liked the sound of that. Perhaps there was a title there . . .

There was a little crowd up ahead, perhaps six people, standing and listening to a man who stood atop a wooden box, lecturing in a strident, resonant voice to any and all who walked by.

The lecturer wore a black suit with a high collar, and his eyes were as piercingly black as his skin. He seemed to be a creature of the night, and Benny could not guess his age. He had seemed old when Benny had first seen him as a boy, old when they had bumped into each other at the fair, and old when Benny had returned from the war, thinking of shattered bodies and death, and dreaming of freedom. Old.

And old now. But not looking that much older. He was known the neighborhood over simply as The Preacher, and he was in fine form this night.

He roared out to them: "And he said to me: These words are trustworthy and true. And the Lord, the God of the spirits of the prophets, has sent his angel, has sent his angel to show his servants what must soon take place."

"Amen, Brother," someone in the little crowd said.

"Preach it!" said another.

The words had a kind of dreamy quality, as if Benny had heard them before, long ago in another place. The Preacher pointed at Benny as he approached, and some of the people in the crowd turned to look, curious. "Then the eyes of the blind shall be opened, and the ears of the deaf shall be unstopped." He said, "Praise the Lord, open their eyes. Help them to see!"

Confused, Benny tapped a forefinger on his own chest. "Are you talking to me?"

"Oh, that my words were now written! Oh, that they were printed in a book!" His eyes burned, and narrowed as he gazed at Benny. "Write those words, Brother Benny. Let them see the glory of what lies ahead."

"I've never understood," Benny said, laughing in spite of his confusion. "How do you know who everybody is? What we do? Who we are?"

"I see, Brother Benny. I have always seen. It is the curse and the blessing of the Prophets so to do."

Benny looked at the old man's eyes blazing from age-hollowed sockets. And finally, all he could do was nod. "All right, man. It's cool."

"Go now, and write the truth that's in your heart. The truth that 'shall set them free!'" The Preacher gave Benny a last hard look, and Benny went on his way.

Strange about the old man: You might see him once a week, or once a year. No one knew where he lived, but he seemed to know everything, and everyone. Somehow, his words both disturbed and comforted Benny, and as he watched the old man walk away, his mind played its trick on him again. And the old man looked like . . . he saw in the old man's eyes . . .

Joseph Sisko. Yes. The father of Benjamin Sisko, the space station commander.

Father? Benny had barely known his own father. How odd to look at this wild creature, this thing of the streets, and think of him as someone's father.

The truth shall set them free . . .

"Hallelujah," Benny said quietly. And finished the rest of the walk to his apartment.

Benny's apartment was a small, shabby one-room hole-in-the-wall. But it was his, and it was home. Books were crammed everywhere, cluttered everywhere, along with a rich and varied collection of native African artifacts. He loved collecting them, and thought the obsession had something to do with that World's Fair exhibit he had seen, so long ago.

Hung on his living room wall to the right of his desk was a Dogon door, barrier against evil spirits. A Zulu medicine mask graced the wall nearby, and another Dogon artifact, a burial urn shaped like a bird, sat somberly on a kitchen shelf.

His Remington and a radio sat on the kitchen table, near the window. Articles on astronomy and physics were pinned on the walls everywhere, and a periodic table of the elements was fastened to the icebox by a round magnet. There were a few cheaply framed *Incredible Tales* covers, all prominently featuring illustrations of his own stories. An Earth globe hung suspended from the ceiling above his desk, low enough to study as reference. It was cozy on a good day, cramped on a bad. Regardless of which it was at any given time, it was definitely home.

He turned on the radio and diddled the dial while the tubes warmed up, faint sounds at first, growing louder slowly, and he dialed until he found something familiar—the sweet, warbling sax of Charlie Parker. It was like balm on scalded nerves.

He walked over to the upright piano over in the

corner, and he sat down at the bench. The piano's surface was marred and scuffed, but as he flipped the lid up and began to run his fingers over the keys, it responded as if it understood loss, but had never known it.

It had been his father's, the only thing left behind when "Fox" Russell disappeared. Then it belonged to his mother, who died soon afterwards. Then his aunt, who was his only family in the world and who had passed just last year, leaving the piano to him.

He rested his head on his hands. He couldn't go down that lane. He just couldn't. But he could take that pain, he could take that loss, and he could do the only thing that he knew which could stop the anguish. He could give it to one of his characters and, through working of the story, show how they had managed to turn travail into power. Show how they had grown in spite of their loss. It was his most powerful weapon. It would not fail him now.

He pushed himself away from the piano. He might be alone in the world, but he was not the only one who felt so, and perhaps it was the task of the writer, of the artist, to take human pain and transform it into understanding.

Well, then . . . who in his story might have suffered loss? He couldn't give the character loss without triumph. That was unfair to his readers. Too many of them had known loss. It was his job to help them to make sense of their lives, or at least to honestly try to make sense of his own, and then put the results, whatever they might be, onto paper.

It was the Captain, it was this man Sisko who had

known loss. Yes. He had lost his wife . . . on the Space Station? No. He had lost his wife on another station, where he had served, during an enemy attack. There had been . . . fire . . . and death, and he had been helpless to save her.

With an unsteady hand, Benny rolled a sheet of paper into the carriage. He looked at the paper, and then began to type:

Captain Benjamin Sisko sat looking out the window of Deep Space Nine, *his ebony reflection staring back at him. There was a job to do, but as with all men, sometimes memories of the past intruded upon the present. These memories were painful. Any memory of the only woman he had ever loved was painful. And yet he would not have given them up for all the Tarkelean Tea in the Galaxy . . .*

Benny typed for almost an hour without stopping, finding his way into another world, a world where the faucets did not leak, where the paper-thin walls did not conduct the sound of the nightly, vicious domestic quarrel from the neighboring apartment. Where racist cops didn't roust men just for breathing their precious air. He slipped deeper and deeper into a world where honor and intelligence and courage were the measure of a being—whether human or alien, male or female. Black or white. A better world than the one in which he lived.

When he looked up, there was a half-inch stack of paper on the table before him. He had fed sheet after sheet into the typewriter without thinking. He glanced at his watch: it was after midnight. He really should be thinking about bedtime. He really should.

But then Benny looked over into the window, and saw something that, despite his fatigue, despite his weariness, made him smile. The image, in his mind, was not that of Benny Russell, middle-aged Negro science fiction writer. No Ralph Ellison. No Richard Wright. Perhaps a hack, but a *sincere* hack, and that had to be worth something.

No, what he saw in the window was a proud black man wearing a Starfleet uniform. A man who had never bowed. Who had known loss but not defeat, depression but not despair.

Benjamin Sisko. Starfleet officer.

Benny took a deep breath, regaining more than his composure. He had regained, just for that precious moment, his identity.

With renewed energy, he began to type. His fingers struck the keys in a blur, tirelessly, long into the night, long after the couple next door had stopped arguing, until the only sound in the entire building was the steady, burring slap of cast-iron typeface against white paper.

SHUFFLE

CHAPTER
13

1940

MR. COOLEY and his group found their way to the amusements area, where Benny was guided away from the dancing girl shows. ("I don't think those white men would greatly appreciate Negro boys looking at those half-naked white girls" Cooley said. Little Cassie was more direct and explicit about it and expressed, strongly, the opinion that there wouldn't be anything in there worth seeing at all.)

Despite stupendous crowds, through a fluke they actually managed to catch one of Robinson's musical shows. A rumor ran through the mob that Mae West was appearing at the main pavilion. It was considered possible—that stage had seen Abbott and Costello and the Marx Brothers earlier in the week. As it turned out, that had been a false rumor, but it did thin the crowd for the music theater. Cooley's class, including Benny, Jenny, and Cassie, had been able to find seats. When the curtain went up, for the next forty minutes Benny was thrilled more than he would have believed possible by the dancing of the legendary Bill "Bojangles" Robinson. Never in his life had he seen such an exhibition of grace and ease of motion, and for just an instant, he craved the fluidity of dance for himself, craved to be able to move with the kind of ease men like Robinson and Willie Hawkins displayed so effortlessly.

He looked over at Jenny and was just a little lost at the way she gazed at Robinson, felt searing envy that mere dancing could wring that kind of response from a woman. What would he have to have, what would he have to *do* before he could ever hope to trigger such admiration? He didn't know, but he knew that he wanted it.

Somewhere inside him there was something special. He knew it, and if he just had a chance, he would be able to find it. He knew that, too.

He was almost out of money, and Jenny had begun complaining that her feet were sore. The other kids were starting to get restless too. They had gone by the Hall of Nations twice, and the exhibit had still been closed. Cooley had managed to find them other things to do, things to fill up their time, but Benny had begun to doubt that Cooley would be able to keep them in good spirits long enough to get them to the exhibition, assuming of course that the exhibition would even open.

So they were on their way out of the fair, when he

convinced them to walk the long blocks necessary to see the Hall of Nations, one last time.

Complaining and grousing—the fair was an entire small world, it seemed—they went, and much to their surprise, when they got there, it was actually open.

The Hall of Nations was a long white building—there were actually two of them, on either side of the Lagoon of Nations, a sparkling blue pool that never seemed to stop its shimmering and bubbling. It was near the Court of Peace, and the stepped waterfall of Italy's exhibit. The lagoon itself was eight hundred by four hundred feet and looked big enough to drown Rockefeller Center.

So. This was where the poorer Nations hung up their shingle, he thought. Not bad, but it would have been wonderful if one of the African nations had a proud pavilion like even Poland had.

But at least it wasn't represented by a little grass hut, or something. Images of natives capering around a roasting missionary, or Tarzan of the Apes rescuing a blond from a crowd of ravening native savages. That would have been a little much.

But the inside of the Hall of Nations was tasteful, if rather quiet. There was an exhibit from Yugoslavia, one from Panama, and another from Siam. Cooley led them quickly through it, and back to one of the nooks, where he finally found the exhibit from the Mali Republic.

It was labeled, simply, "Dogon Artifact."

There was a curtain across an alcove, and an irregular radiance pulsing from behind it. A withered little black man sat on a stool, looking out at them as if doing a mental count, as if he were hoarding his remaining life energy, waiting for a critical mass of bodies to arrive before beginning his spiel.

Benny looked at them, and then at a tapestry on one of the walls. Clearly, Mali (wherever *that* was) had little money to invest. He actually figured that there was a good chance that this little man had expended most of his money just getting here.

The twelve students slid along a bend, and waited for the curator to begin. Then finally, he stood, and in a very thick accent began to speak.

"Hello," he said. "I am Ajabwe. I come from Mali in Africa. My people, a great people, are the Dogon." He paused. "The legend says that many years ago my people were visited by a strange folk, who came from another star. It was said that they traveled in search of those who could understand, and that only a very small number of people could understand the gift that they offered. They said that they traveled in search of the few who had this, and when they found it, they would leave one of the Orbs with which they were entrusted. I do not know if the story is true, or how much of it is true—but it is said that these people either represented, or called themselves the Prophets." He looked out at them, and Benny had to admit that his smile was a little unnerving.

"Perhaps one of you will be a Chosen One." Some of the white people in the audience chuckled, but not impolitely.

He opened the curtain.

The light flickered more strongly, and the breath froze in Benny's throat. The object behind the curtain was, simply, beautiful. Waves of blue fire rolled off of it like mist from a chunk of dry ice. The glow grew more and more intense, and he couldn't feel himself breathe, or even really think.

They rose from the seats and filed past, prevented from approaching the strange shape by a velvet rope. It was, as they had said in the paper, about the size and shape of a large hourglass, thicker through the middle, of course, and that light. That light . . .

He stared at it. Benny closed his eyes tightly, as if trying to keep the luminescence from washing through him, but it was of no use. It ignored his eyelids, as if it was radiating directly into his brain.

Something . . . something was shifting deep within the orb, and he heard it, and it seemed to speak to him.

But the words that it said were beyond him. He couldn't quite make them out . . . they stayed, remained just beyond his reach and his understanding.

Then he was falling, and falling. The world seemed to open up, and he was lost.

"Benny?" he heard, but couldn't see anything at all.

"Benny, are you all right?" It was Jenny. She was calling to him. She was waking him up, and that meant that he must be sleeping and dreaming, but the dream had been so strange. He had had a brief, but brilliant vision that seemed like the Flash Gordon serials he had seen as a boy—only realer. Scary real, as real as the cars rolling down the street. That real.

Benny opened his eyes, and he saw Jenny and

Cassie standing over him and Mr. Cooley, with an expression of genuine concern behind his spectacles.

"What . . . what happened?" Benny said groggily.

"That's what I would like to know," Cooley said.

Benny sat up, and felt the dizziness begin to recede. He shook his head and realized that the old African man Ajabwe was looking at him, too. Ajabwe, who seemed puzzled, asked: "Who are you, boy?"

"Benny Russell?" Benny said.

"Well, Benny Russell, I think that the gem has spoken to you."

"What?"

"It happened once before. A tall man, in robes. He said that he was a preacher. Are you a preacher?"

"No," Benny said, confused.

"I think that perhaps you are a leader in some way. The gem has spoken to you." He said this last as if it answered all questions.

Benny rose unsteadily to his feet. The little man helped him up. Ajabwe's skin was warm and dry. Despite Benny's initial unease, he could not dislike this man.

"You come back," the little old man said. "You come back and see me, and the stone—again."

There was no answer that Benny could make, except to nod his head dumbly. He really couldn't do anything other than agree.

The trip back to Harlem was uneventful. The entire group seemed to be somewhat subdued, perhaps by what had happened at the fair, perhaps something else. They seemed both solicitous of Benny and simultaneously rather wary of him. He couldn't figure it out—he had just collapsed, not displayed the symptoms of some terrible, infectious disease.

"Why are they treating me like that?" he finally asked Cooley.

"Like what?"

"Like I'm Typhoid Mary or something? It's kind of spooky."

Cooley gazed at him for a long moment before answering. "It probably has something to do with the way you were talking," he said.

"Talking? I don't know what you mean."

Cooley just gazed at him, and didn't say anything else.

Jenny rested back against her seat, her eyes closed, long dark lashes quivering slightly.

Only Cassie was still awake, alert, and watching him. "Cassie?" he asked. "What was that all about?"

"You were saying things, Benny."

"What kind of things?"

She shrugged. "It didn't really make no sense."

"Then tell me what it was."

"Well, you were talking about the stars. You were saying that you could see the stars. That's all."

Benny closed his eyes. The blackness behind them was filled with something that he had never glimpsed before. It was blackness, and a roiling series of clouds, and exploding stars, and out among them, men and women and other things. Creatures. But not monsters. Machines. Holes in space. He suddenly felt a lifting and turning within himself, a humming, as if he had touched some primal dynamo at the very core of creation.

He opened his eyes again. The train still made its rickety way along the track. "Cass?" he said softly.

"Yeah?" For a moment her tough-girl exterior had cracked and he saw something underneath it. And then . . .

He saw not Cass, but Cassie. She was grown up and beautiful. And she knew about makeup and dressing, and she held her arms out to him, and—

He felt something hot boiling within his blood, and he shook his head quickly. What the hell had *that* vision been about? He was imagining that he saw Cass, not as she was, but as she might be in another ten or fifteen years. That was crazy.

She held his hand. "Yes? Was there something?"

He shook his head. "No." He paused and then realized that that was a lie. "Cassie," he said. "When we were in the tent, didn't you see anything at all?"

"Nothing," she said. And then settled her head back against the seat. Without opening her eyes she said, "Nothing at all."

SHUFFLE

CHAPTER
14

1953

TIME PASSED, days which were for Benny Russell among the best he had ever known. Wrapped in a cocoon of words, of images, of sounds and sensations that no one on Earth could create or understand but him, he wrote and wrote and wrote. Never had the words flowed so smoothly, so naturally, until it seemed that the story was telling itself to him, until it seemed that his fingers were just an electrical conduit and that through them flowed something which was not *from* Benny Russell, but *of* him.

He felt like a painter might, who merely scraped primer off a canvas to find a masterpiece underneath. It was not work. It was something else.

Celebration, perhaps.

He needed little sleep, little food. He spurned the bed and simply drowsed for a few minutes at his desk, lost in the world that unfolded itself to him.

Oh, in earlier stories he had written about a strange and strangely heuristic universe of the future, filled with creatures that had names vaguely familiar and simultaneously strange. He had written of adventures on far planets and of several tales of a Captain named Kirk who, bolder than most, went into the jaws of danger beside his crew, buckling every swash in sight. When readers complained that a *real* captain wouldn't place himself in such constant danger, he made a shift, wrote of another starship, where the captain and the captain's primary officer shared responsibility, and these stories found an even greater audience.

And he had, upon occasion, slipped in a man or woman of his own skin color. A communications officer. A blind ensign. Even a wise woman of seemingly endless empathy. And he loved those scenes. But always, and ever, the primary responsibilities lay with those white people who captained the ship.

Now, for the very first time, he was writing a tale about a man who looked like him, and the difference was startling. He had loved Kirk, and Picard—but he *was* Sisko. He could feel this man's pain, he could share his dreams. Sisko's triumphs and struggles called to the very deepest parts of Benny, made him consider every word in a manner he had never done before, made him strive to have every action, every thought and sensation not just honest but unique to both character and situation.

This was not just the best work he had ever done.

This was the work he had been born to do, and he knew it.

And soon, so would the entire world.

Sometime on the fifth day, Benny Russell roused himself from a near-somnambulant state and stared at the paper. At some point during the night, only half-aware, he had written "the end" in lowercase letters at the bottom of the page, rolled the sheet out of the typewriter, then simply lay his head in his arms and fallen into unconsciousness. After perhaps five hours of sleep in that fashion, he had awakened, and zombie-walked to his bed, where he fell upon it and slept like the dead. All day and into the following evening he slept.

He arose that second night, and levered himself up. Certainly he had just had a dream. Certainly he hadn't really worked as he imagined he had. Hadn't he actually blistered his way through almost a hundred pages of paper in half that many hours?

But then what was that neat stack of paper sitting beside his typewriter?

It was a thick stack, and he regarded it with almost superstitious awe, not quite certain how to approach it. He brewed his coffee with one eye on the paper as if it might disappear if he blinked too hard or turned away.

He sat and watched the paper, still not quite certain what to think, wondering if gremlins might have appeared in the middle of the night, unbidden, to perform this awesome task. The coffee boiled, and at last he poured himself a cup, then sat by the window and drank it slowly, listening to the sound of cars down outside his window. Finally, after almost ten more minutes had passed, he picked up the first page and began to read.

Eva's Kitchen was a coffee shop on the corner of Lenox and 135th. It had been there for twenty years, serving up its steady diet of strong coffee and tender burgers, grilled lovingly by the big, soft woman who had owned it ever since buying it from its original owner. Rumor said that Eva had been a crackerjack clarinet player—some said that she had played with the Duke himself—until a fight, over a man of course, had smashed her mouth and ruined her embouchure.

The rumor went further to say that the other woman had ended up in the morgue. Slinging hash, in comparison, seemed a good deal.

In her prime, Big Eva Cunningham had been a sloe-eyed Mississippi beauty who even close to sixty years old (as she simply *had* to be), still had the ability to turn heads and draw wolf whistles on the occasions when she exposed a few inches of those fine brown legs.

Benny's mouth began to water when Eva's Kitchen came into view, anticipating his favorite breakfast, and even more, anticipating a conversation with the woman who would serve it. He felt tired—in some ways more fatigued than he could remember feeling, but in others, he felt better than he had in years.

In a thick manila envelope beneath his right arm, he held his masterwork, and life just didn't get much better than that.

The restaurant was busy, as it always was, but he saw an empty seat at the counter and took it swiftly and quietly, aware that the counter girl had yet to spot him.

This was bliss. He had the opportunity to watch the waitress without her awareness, an opportunity to enjoy the simple sight and sound of her, and he always reveled in that.

She was five foot eight of brown sugar, with the sweetest hips imaginable, and legs that had been created on a sex fiend's lathe. Her hair was up, and fairly straight. He always felt a bit of irritation at this. It was the style, but she spent too many hours straightening her hair. She had "good" hair, and she enjoyed taking advantage of that and enjoyed flaunting it at every opportunity.

She was a brown-skinned woman, generous of smile and laughter, simple in her tastes, loyal and warmhearted. And, he knew, she loved him.

If he was very, very lucky, he would find his way to loving her as well, given time. He hoped so. A woman like this wouldn't wait forever.

"Hey, Baby," she said, finally spotting him. "Have a seat." She reached across the counter, and took his hand. "The usual?"

He shook his head negative. "How about scrambling the eggs today, Cassie?"

As he watched her, that odd feeling came over him

again. Suddenly, the rest of the grill seemed to disappear, and he saw her standing there in a jumpsuit of sorts, obviously a product of the same era he had described in his story. She was the same, but different. No more beautiful . . . perhaps more self-confident. And her name was . . .

Kasidy Yates

She was the woman who had stolen Benjamin Sisko's heart. He smiled to himself, slightly. The character of Kasidy Yates had yet to appear in his story, but he knew that after he sold this one, there would be another, and then another, and that Sisko would eventually meet Kasidy Yates, and that they would fall in love.

"My," she said. "Aren't we feeling adventurous."

She poured him a cup of coffee. He was simply bursting to give her his news. Finally he extracted the envelope from beneath his arm, slapping it on the counter in front of him. "It's done," he said proudly.

"What is it?" Her eyes were gentle, unmocking, genuinely curious.

"Only the best story I've ever written."

She kissed him with a smile. "That's great, baby," she said. "I got some good news, too." She leaned forward, placing one of her hands over his. She looked him in the eye and when she spoke, it was with great sincerity.

"I talked to Mrs. Jackson last night," she said. "She's serious about retiring in the next couple years. I asked her about selling this place to us and she said she'd be willing." She was almost bubbling with the news and he knew why. Eva's Kitchen meant security. It meant a future. And by sharing this news with him, he realized what she was actually saying.

He cleared his throat uncomfortably. "Cassie, we've been over this. I *have* a job. I'm a writer."

The warmth in her expression never flagged. God, this was a good woman, and they had known each other all their lives. "And how much money have you earned doing that?"

He turned his palms up. "I've only been working at it for a few years."

Her smile flattened slightly. "A few years? More like fifteen, if you count all those stories you wrote in the Navy."

He shrugged. "That was amateur stuff."

For just these moments, she had forgotten that there were other customers in the shop. Her expression was all love, all understanding. It reminded him of his mother's, and that, somehow, was the worst thing of all. "Baby," she said, "Neither one of us is getting any younger. Don't you see? This is our chance. We can make some money. Get married. You're always writing about the future—well, look around—this is *our* future."

She meant that kindly, lovingly, but it was difficult for Benny to take it in that spirit. He looked around and saw the customers. They were the same ones he had seen here in Eva's on and off for the past ten years. There was the fat truck driver over there, having his morning coffee, and Ozzie, who ran the barber shop just behind him. A couple of local churchwomen, probably having breakfast before attending one function meeting or another, and a few of the girls who worked sewing clothes over a couple of blocks out.

It was the usual crowd, and he liked them. As far as they knew him, they liked him as well. Yet, he knew that there was some part of him that would wither if he accepted her offer. Conversely, there was some part of her, the girl who still lived within the woman, which would wither if he wasn't able to answer. He really wanted to. In fact, he couldn't precisely say exactly *why* he was having so much trouble.

Before he could say anything, there was a commotion behind him, followed by a chorus of "Way to go, Willie!" and "Good game!" and "Way to go, my man," and a "You showed them bums" from the other customers. There was a sprinkling of applause as the door opened, and Willie Hawkins ambled in.

Hawkins was tall, dark, commanding, a prince in his own kingdom. As with Cassie, Benny had known Willie all of his life, and had always, from the very beginning, known that Willie was headed for something good. Willie ran too fast, hit too far, wrestled too hard—the boy was a natural athlete who had boxed, and run track, and played varsity baseball. It was this last which had captured professional notice, and ultimately paid his ticket.

He wore a stylish suit right now, with a silver-tipped walking cane, a silk shirt stretched across his impressive chest, and a hundred-watt smile that he had turned full-bore on Cassie.

As well dressed as he was—as he always was, so that his fur-lined coats and walking stick could be spotted a block away—this wasn't the dress that got him the most attention. It was when Willie wore the uniform of a New York Yankee that he drew the most attention. He was a star, had fulfilled all of the hopes and dreams of those who had watched him grow up. He had been only the fourth Negro player ever signed by the major leagues, and every home run, every catch, every out, hell, every *bunt* was a personal victory for the folks in Harlem, and they loved him.

He sauntered up to the counter, and as he did, again, Benny had a flash, another of those bizarre mental anomalies. He had written characters before, only later to realize that they were based on people he already knew. But never had he had so many of them, in such a short period of days.

Willie, boisterous, jovial, athletic "Willie the Warrior" he was often called, suddenly seemed less human, less handsome. Almost grotesque, and yet . . . even his imagination's attempt to discount Willie seemed to backfire. In this new guise, ridges across his nose, wearing an alien uniform, he wasn't less attractive. He was somehow almost super-humanly virile. And his . . . and his name was . . .

Worf.

Yes, that was it. His name was Worf. And he was a . . . Klingon. Yes. But not a villain. In this new universe, old enemies had become new friends. Now, Worf was an ally.

"Hey, there, Cassie," Willie said. "Hear the game last night? I went two for four and robbed Snider of a tater. You shoulda heard the crowd yell!"

"Sure they were yelling," Benny said mildly. "They want to know why the Giants are in fifth place."

Willie looked at Benny with an old and practiced ill humor. "Cassie," he said. "Why don't you tell this fool to take his business someplace else?"

She smiled, and her smile was pure sugar. "I've thought about it," she said. "Trouble is, if he did leave, he'd take my heart with him."

Willie shrugged his massive shoulders. "Ask me, you're wasting an awfully pretty heart."

Cassie looked at Benny. "I don't think so."

Benny reached over and squeezed her hand. "Strike three, Willie," he said. "You're out."

Willie smiled slyly. "That's awright," he said, letting the words just slide past his tongue. "I'll get another turn at bat."

One of the other customers paid his tab and left, and Willie sat down. "Now . . . how about frying me up some steak and eggs?"

"Coming right up," Cassie said. "But first, tell me something. How come you're still living up here in Harlem? I mean, a famous ballplayer like you can live anywhere."

"The hell I can," Willie said amiably. "They can hardly get used to me playing alongside them on the ball field. Living next to 'em . . . that's a whole other story."

Benny just bet. In his opinion—not that anyone was going to ask for it—Willie's other motivation was that here, in Harlem, he was more than a star. He was King. If by some miracle he was able to move into a white neighborhood, he'd just be that uppity nigger ballplayer.

Willie wanted to be a huge fish in a small pond.

Willie was still talking, and he might have been reading Benny's mind. "Besides—around here, when people look at me, it's 'cause they admire me. There, I'm just another colored boy who can hit a curve ball."

He paused and laughed, but Benny suddenly knew why he liked Willie, in spite of his ego, in spite of the obvious fact that he would like to wiggle his way in-between him and Cassie. Willie was perfectly aware of the world that he lived in. Despite his bluster, he had a dose of self-awareness that sometimes caught Benny by surprise. Willie was no fool. He was using the skills he had, doing the best he could, and taking the hisses and the threats—

(What was that joke? "Baseball is the only place in the world where a nigger can wave a stick at a white man and not get lynched . . .")

—and paying back the bigots is the only way society lets him—on the diamond.

And for that, Benny had to admire him.

Willie looked over and saw a gaggle of girls at another table waving at him.

"Now, if you'll excuse me," he said, smoothing back his processed hair. "My public awaits." He prowled over to the girls and flashed them his winning smile.

Cassie watched him, and Benny watched her do it, wondering if there wasn't some part of her that wondered what it would be like to be Willie's woman.

116

Benny was wondering if she thought for even a minute that Willie could be sincere, that she could win and keep Willie's love, would she leave Benny?

"I'll see to those eggs," she said gently, and it took him a moment to realize that she was talking to him, gazing at him as if she were able to read his mind, and wanted to ease his fears.

She mimed a kiss to him, then she moved off toward the kitchen. He heard her give her order to Eva, and he saw the owner's head bobbing happily around as she performed her magic. Wasn't nobody for twenty blocks could burn an egg like Eva.

A skinny kid with smart wide eyes slid up to the counter next to Benny as he sipped at his coffee and began to read his newspaper. "Hey, Benny," the kid said. "Wanna buy a watch—"

Benny turned to look at him, and time froze.

It was happening again. This boy is . . . his name is Jimmy I've known him since he was in diapers. But he's more than that. He's, he's . . .

Benny rubbed at his temples, confused, wondering for just a moment what he was doing, just what the hell was going on.

Then the name came to him. *Jake Sisko.* He's the son of Benjamin Sisko, the thing the intrepid commander of DS9 loves most in all the world—

Benny shook himself out of it. The watch was only a Timex, but it wasn't the cheapest model. Benny had a strong suspicion that there was a five-and-dime someplace with an empty spot in its showcase.

"Where'd you get that?" he asked.

"I found it. Nice, huh?" Jimmy smiled toothily.

Benny was almost overwhelmed with a rush of emotion. He liked this kid. "One of these days, Jimmy," he said, "you're going to find yourself in serious trouble."

Jimmy wagged his head, too smart for his own good. "Anything I can get into, I can get out of."

"You keep thinking that—see what happens."

"Man," Jimmy said. "How come you're always lecturing me?"

"I'm not lecturing you," Benny said. "I'm trying to help you."

Jimmy's eyes narrowed. "You want to help me, buy this watch. I could use the cash."

Benny sighed. "Why not get a job?"

"As what? A delivery boy or a dishwasher? No, thanks. I like being my own boss. Setting my own hours."

Benny fought back a flash of anger, but was unable to completely keep the sarcasm from his voice. "Sounds like a great life."

The small touch of camaraderie between them, the sliver of vulnerability in Jimmy vanished. Benny could see it retreat as if a steel door had suddenly slammed down. "Yours ain't no better," he said. "Writing stories about a bunch of white people living on the moon. Who cares about that?"

Who indeed? a voice inside Benny whispered.

"I'm not doing that anymore," Benny said. "I'm writing about us."

Jimmy's expression had gone from borderline anger to humorous incredulity in a heartbeat. "You mean about colored people on the moon? Bullshit, man. Never happen."

"Check out next month's issue," Benny said conspiratorially.

Something flickered in Jimmy's eyes, something that Benny suspected was genuine amusement. "A coon on the moon?"

"That's not the words I'd use. But we're there."

"All right, man—you're on. Maybe I'll check that out. Which means . . ."

"Which means?"

"That I'm gonna need to raise some cash. Anyway, got business. Later."

He slid off the stool and began to stroll the diner again, seeking customers.

He knew that Jimmy didn't believe him. But that was all right. He had the proof. He had the best story he'd ever done. Maybe Willie didn't accept it. And maybe Cassie, who loved him, couldn't quite share in his vision. But for the first time in years Benny had that feeling, the feeling that his fingers were on fire, that there was someone sitting on his shoulder telling him the story. He was absolutely burning up, and he knew that this story was going to do it. This story was going to change everything.

CHAPTER
15

THE OFFICES WERE QUIET, and had been since the first preliminary reading had begun. Benny had gone outside, walked around, come back, paced, gone outside again.

And finally sat, and decided that it might be best if he simply resolved to take his medicine like a man.

He had run out of fingernails to chew, and begun considering his knuckles.

Herbert Rossoff sat at the table, completely engrossed as he read a carbon copy of a novella-sized manuscript. As he finished a sheet and began to read the next, he handed the finished page over to Kay, who was seated next to him.

Judging by her reaction—she barely seemed to be breathing—Kay was so completely involved in reading that she hadn't enough concentration left over to even chew her doughnut.

As she finished her page and continued on to the next, she handed off her sheet to Julius. Julius moved his lips when he read, something that Herbert usually ribbed him about, but today, no one noticed anyone's affectations. When Albert finished a page, he handed off to Ritterhouse.

When Ritterhouse finished he passed it up to a woman standing behind them. The woman was Darlene Kursky, and she was part of the reason that Benny had left the room. She was just too damned similar to the way he had envisioned a bizarre character named Dax, a binary life form—a humanoid female with an ancient, symbiotic being implanted in her abdomen.

That amused him, because as she read it, her brow furrowed in concentration. "She has a worm in her belly?" Darlene said. "That's disgusting." She paused for a moment. "Interesting, but disgusting."

The other writers looked at her, speechless for a baffled beat, as if they were trying to place her. Albert was the first to speak. "Who . . . what is, if you don't mind me asking . . . are, uh . . ."

She laughed. "I'm Mister Pabst's new secretary. Darlene Kursky." She pointed to the manuscript. "Which one of you wrote this?"

"I did," Benny said.

"You?"

"Surprise."

She shook her head in admiration. "It's the best thing I've read since 'The Puppet Masters.'" She paused, and he had the feeling that she was being almost apologetic. "I read a lot of science fiction," she finally said.

"Bless you, my child," Herbert said fervently.

Kay chimed in right on cue. "The world needs more people like you," she said.

Albert turned to Benny. He had always liked Benny's writing, but there was newfound respect in his eyes. "The story really . . . I mean to say . . ." he just couldn't seem to get the words out. "It's quite . . . impressive."

"It's a damn fine piece of writing is what it is," Herbert said. His eyes shone. "And 'Deep Space Nine' is a very intriguing title."

"Very admirable," Julius said.

Herbert couldn't resist reinterpreting Julius's thoughts. "The master of understatement," he said. "What he really means is that he wishes he had half your talent."

"I really like this major of yours," Kay said. "She's a tough cookie."

He almost, but not quite laughed when she said this, his imagination filling in the pieces. Of *course* she would like Major Kira. In his mind, that is who Kay was. The ridged nose, the earring, everything.

"There aren't enough strong women characters in science fiction. I'm always saying that, aren't I, Jules?"

"Ad nauseam, my dear."

Roy was rereading some of the middle passages. "These Cardassians . . . I like how you've described them. Their neck ridges especially. I'll come up with some sketches to show you. It could make a nice cover."

But before Benny could answer, a voice boomed in from back in the offices. It was Pabst. "Don't waste your time," he said.

They all turned in time to see Pabst emerge from his office, holding the original of Benny's story. He pointed a stubby finger at Darlene. "You, back to work."

"Right away, Mister Pabst." She scurried back to her desk.

"You too Roy."

Roy gave Benny a shrug of defeat, and then left the room.

Herbert regarded Pabst with suspicion. "Douglas— you're not going to stand there and tell us you don't like this story." His expression, his carriage . . . he was virtually daring his editor to say this very thing.

"Oh, I like it all right. It's good. Very good."

He crossed over to Benny. Benny felt as if he was holding his breath.

"However . . . you know that I can't print it."

Benny swallowed. "Why not?" The lie was implicit in the words. He knew damned well why Pabst couldn't print it. He just wanted to hear it.

"Come on, Benny," Pabst said, the very soul of reason. "Your hero's a Negro captain. The head of a space station, for Christ's sake."

"What's wrong with that?" Something large and hot was stirring behind Benny's eyes, something creating pressure that would build and build. So far, he was keeping it under control, but in all honesty he wasn't certain how long he would be able to continue.

"People won't accept it," Pabst said. "It's not believable."

"And men from Mars are?" Herbert said. For once, Benny was happy for Rossoff's acid wit.

Pabst brushed the challenge off. "Stay out of this, Herb." He turned back to Benny.

Benny wished that he could have looked at the man and objected to something that existed in his carriage. He wished there was some antagonism, some glee in the pain he was causing a man who was, if not a friend, at least a compatriot. "Look, Benny—I'm a magazine editor, not a crusader. I'm not here to change society or rock the boat in any way. I'm here to put out a magazine. That's my job. And that means I've got to answer to Mister Stone, the national distributors, the wholesalers . . ."

Pabst held up the story, the precious sheaf of paper that Benny had labored over for so long. Not an hour ago, he had been certain those pages constituted the best and most powerful work of his life. Now he was wondering if they were the worst mistake he had ever made.

Pabst leaned closer. "And none of them are going to want to put this on the newsstand. For all we know, it could cause a race riot."

He said this with awesome conviction, and Benny expected the room to go dead silent. Instead, the regular, ironic sound of Herbert's bitter applause echoed in the room.

"Congratulations, Douglas," Herbert said. "That's the most imbecilic attempt to rationalize personal cowardice that I've ever heard."

"Oh-uh," Kay said. "He's angry now."

"Herb's been angry ever since Joseph Stalin died," Pabst said snidely.

Herbert shot to his feet. "What's that supposed to mean?" His face darkened with anger.

"You know exactly what it means," Pabst assured him.

"You calling me a red?" Herbert had balled his fists up, and was virtually in midair when Benny stepped between them. "Whoa. Easy," Benny said.

Julius seemed a little shaken by it all. "Calm down, dear boy. We're writers, not Vikings."

Herbert's face, if not his politics, remained red. He wanted blood. "I'm not going to let some craven fascist call me a pinko and get away from it."

Rather lamely, Benny thought, Albert tried to change the direction of the discussion by focusing the attention on himself. "Douglas," he said. "What'd you . . . uh . . . think of *my* story?"

"I loved it," Pabst said soothingly. Oil on troubled waters, that was Pabst. "You see, Albert's got the right idea. He's not interested in Negroes or whites—he writes about robots."

"That's because he *is* a robot," Herbert said. "No offense, Albert."

"I . . . uh, like robots. They're very . . . efficient."

The mood in the office was ghastly. The vilest insult match ever engaged in by Rossoff and Julius Eaton had never chilled the mood this badly. This was real, and it was bloody, and Benny was stuck right in the middle of it.

Pabst made another attempt to heal the whole

thing, to patch it before their little band of jolly comrades was irreparably ruptured. He grabbed a new illustration of Roy's from the table. This one depicted a family being sold a used rocket ship by a particularly oily salesman. He offered the drawing to Benny.

"Here," Pabst said, his tone remarkably similar to the one the salesman might have used. "Write me a novella based on this drawing and I'll print it in next month's issue. Do a good job and you might even get the cover."

Benny looked at it. Actually, it was a good illustration. His nimble mind was already playing with ideas.

But somewhere deep within him, there was a voice calling to him. He couldn't bring himself to forget the voice which had sung to him for three nights, the call of his muse. He dared not betray her. "What about my story?" he asked.

Pabst sighed deeply and sincerely. "The way I see it," he said, "you can either burn it or you can put it in a drawer for fifty years or however long it takes the human race to become color-blind."

"But I want people to read it *now.*"

Pabst's voice dropped, became very low, direct, and calm. "You want me to publish it?" he asked. "Then make the captain white."

That last word resounded in the room. They all knew that that was exactly, precisely the truth. And all of them understood what Benny was going to say. "But that's not what I wrote," he said. His voice sounded terribly small, a whisper in a whirlwind.

Pabst shrugged. For him, there was really no debate. In all honesty, the discussion was already over. "It's your decision," he said. Then he turned and headed back into his office.

The others seemed to find things to busy themselves with: paper clips, memos, quiet conversations. Not one of them wanted to intrude on Benny's misery. Not one of them didn't wish to be elsewhere. It is rarely entertaining to watch a friend skinned alive.

Benny looked at the new picture. And at his manuscript. He could write a new story, and give up the work that he had done. But that wouldn't be true to his muse. No one would ever read this story. No one would know how *good* he was. This story would make him, he knew it.

On the other hand, if he changed the captain's race, if he removed Benjamin Sisko's color from the equation, something even worse would happen.

There was a world inside him, a world where a planetary Federation held together a coalition of planets and species. It was a world without poverty, with little crime. With no starvation. With one hundred percent education.

And in a world where humans and Vulcans and Klingons and Bajorans strove to find peace and harmony, the relatively trivial differences between human beings simply meant nothing.

A lovely world.

And Benjamin Sisko, the Federation's finest, a man of intelligence, nerve and decision, was what he was. He was Negro. If Benny changed that, the entire delicate fabric to the universe he had created might collapse, never to resurrect itself. His muse might

CHAPTER
16

1940

IT WAS CLOSE TO ELEVEN by the time that Benny Russell returned home from the Fair. Home was a brownstone walk-up, on East 127th Street, one which might have been comfortable were it shared with his mother and father. But one was dead, and the other gone forever. Benny shared it with his mother's sister Ardelia, a good-hearted woman with an unfortunate addiction to the numbers.

Benny staggered through the front door, feeling unexpectedly weary, calling out: "Ardelia?" and hearing no reply. So—his aunt was still at the policy bank, where she made the majority of her income.

Not a bad business, but an addict like Ardelia needed to put some distance between herself and temptation. Almost any money she made counting slips went right back into her bosses' hands. The rent was currently two months late, and the landlord was screaming bloody murder.

Benny hadn't had time or energy to think about that. He collapsed onto the couch and fell almost immediately into a deep and dream-filled slumber.

Aunt Ardelia was cooking breakfast by the time he awakened, and the smell of bacon and grits filled the apartment. Benny was suddenly and almost overwhelmingly possessed by a ravenous hunger. He rolled clumsily off the couch and thumped onto the floor.

"Ardelia?" he said, pulling his pants on. He hopped his way into the kitchen in time to watch his aunt crack an egg on the side of the skillet.

Ardelia Mathis was a big, brown woman with a generous figure that still resisted gravity admirably. She gave him a big grin and said, "Sit on down, boy, breakfast be up in just a minute. Now, I 'spect you to tell me all about Mr. Bojangles, or you don't even get a bite!"

That sounded like a good deal to him. So in-between huge helpings of steaming grits, eggs so tender they almost melted in his mouth, and bacon that managed to be both crisp and juicy at the same time, he told her all about the fair . . .

Except for the Dogon exhibit. For some reason, he couldn't quite remember anything connected with it, and barely recalled that he had gone there at all.

She listened and laughed, and pursed her mouth into an "O" at his description of the Futurama, and swore that she was going to get out there, she really should, and that she would have some money soon because she just *knew* she was about to hit the number. As she put it, "I just saw a cat get her tail caught in a door, and in Professor Kinder's book, that means my number will be 874." She nodded her head as if this datum was as reliable as the Rock of Gibraltar. "Yes it is."

He sighed. "Was it a male or female cat?" he asked dryly.

"What do you mean?" she asked.

"Was it male or female? Simple question."

She screwed up her face. "Why, I don't know. And why should I?"

"Well, I read the book too, and as I recall—female cats are 874, but male cats are 875."

Her mouth popped into an "o" of surprise, and she dashed off to her bedroom to grab her book and check. Before the heavy sound of her footfalls had faded, he had grabbed another strip of bacon from the pan and skedaddled out of the front door, considering it the better part of valor to vanish before she discovered he was lying.

East 127th Street had been home to Benny for as long as he could remember: he knew the neighborhood like he knew the sound of his own pulse. He could sit on the stoop and tell you when the numbers runners would pass with their policy slips, when the milkman would make his deliveries, when the bakery truck would sputter past.

He knew the barbers and the liquor store owners. He knew the street preachers and the prostitutes.

He was fascinated by the latter, and knew that one day soon he would take the advice of his older, wiser friends, and invest some capital in one of the loudly-dressed, flashy, laughing women who flirted with him, with everyone. After that investment, there would be certain mysteries of life that would be known to him, certain curtains which would remain forever lifted.

Soon, but not today.

He was still confused about what had happened at the Fair, and wasn't certain whether to talk to his friends about it, or just keep it to himself. He certainly couldn't trust his fading memories to Aunt Ardelia—she would just squeal and try to find an entry in one of her dream books that would relate his experience to the upcoming number.

She hadn't always been like this; her world hadn't always revolved around the shadow-land of numbers betting. He remembered when she was a hardworking, loving woman, married to a good man. But she had lost that good man in one of the terrible fires that haunted this neighborhood, one of the roaring blazes over on the border of Spanish Harlem, supposedly started by a Cuban immigrant who didn't understand that you couldn't build a fire in the middle of the floor.

She had lost everything in that blaze, including the only man she loved. He supposed that soon after that she had ceased believing that human dreams or efforts could bend the hand of fate, and just gave in to the worship of blind fortune.

A good woman. Once, a church-going woman.

Now, just someone who gave him a roof to sleep under.

She had already left this morning, heading down to the policy bank, counting slips. Making someone rich. That was just the way of the world. Once, a year ago, she had taken him to her boss man, her work place. It was hidden in a tenement building (hidden—hah! Every cop in town knew where all the policy banks were). It was a room piled high with change, dollar bills, and little slips of paper saying who had bet what and where.

She had worked in one of those joints since before his mother died, even before his Daddy had gone away, following the music that didn't seem to want him any more.

But before that, both Ardelia and her sister, his mother, Emma, had been dancers at the Cotton Club—the Geller sisters, and that was where Emma Geller had met his daddy.

The Cotton Club opened in 1922 at 142nd Street and Lenox Avenue in quarters formerly occupied by the Douglas Casino and the Club Delux. A genteel mobster named Owny Madden ran the club—and half the New York gangs—from a curtained table in the back of the room.

They didn't admit colored customers, but on the stage—the stage!! Such a collection of talent had never been seen in one place at one time before.

Duke Ellington opened there in 1927, debuting his trademarked "jungle sound." He actually recorded some of his best sides right there on the stage. The list of famous names was endless: Ed "Snakehips" Tucker, Evelyn Welch, Bill Robinson, and Buck and Bubbles; the comedian Stepin Fetchit; jazz orchestras led by Cab Calloway, Andrew Preer, Louis Armstrong, and Jimmie Lunceford; the songwriter Harold Arlen; and the singers Lena Horne, Ethel Waters, and Ivie Anderson.

Emma Geller had met her man, "Fox" Russell, at the Cotton Club. Fox was a tall, elegant hipster who played piano for the Duke himself. Emma and "Fox" had mixed like nitro and glycerin, and they'd married in 1923. It was a good time for them, even when the Geller sisters broke up so that Emma could have a child, her only child, Benny. She returned to work two years later, dazzling the crowds with the trademarked steps those girls had practiced since they were six.

But everything changes in this world, and the once glittering crowds began to shrink, perhaps no longer thrilled to take the trip to "Darktown." The declining fortunes of the Cotton Club had influenced the Russell family. Benny's father had started drinking and it had influenced his performance. When the Cotton Club made its move to Broadway and 48th in 1936, "Fox" Russell hadn't gone with it.

Things had gone even worse for his marriage, and it wasn't long before "Fox" didn't have much time for home any more. When he seemed to look forward to his road trips.

Not too much money seemed to make its way back to Benny and his mother. Ardelia found a good man to marry, who forbade her to dance, and was wealthy

enough—he owned real estate in Spanish Harlem—
to keep her in the style she was happy to grow
accustomed to. Ardelia retired, and the dancing duet
called the Geller sisters was history.

By working at a laundry during the day and dancing
where she could at night, Emma was able to keep
things going. Benny offered to drop out to help, but
his mother would have nothing of it. A beautiful,
cream-colored mulatto woman who had once been
courted all over Harlem, she could easily have passed
for white, but hadn't, and now, with Benny as living
testimony to her ethnicity, couldn't.

So Emma tucked away her dreams of glory, or even
comfort and ease, and worked, and worked, and
worked.

And if the poverty and its depravations sometimes
seemed to consume her, she found her comforts in the
church, and her sister's loving marriage.

But when a tenement fire consumed not only Ardelia's husband but most of her financial security, the
sisters seemed to collapse toward a common center.
Each leaned heavily upon the other, and both lost a
little emotional balance. They began to show too
much vulnerability to snake-oil scams, lucky tokens
and pyramid schemes, gambling, lotteries, and every
other way to hold onto some kind of dream that
maybe, someday, somehow, there would be a way out
for their family.

Emma finally broke in 1936, her health failing, and
she died two years later. Benny moved in with
Ardelia.

By this point Ardelia gambled so regularly that the

runners all knew her, and when one of the higher-ups heard that she had pawned her wedding ring to raise money, they finally offered her a job.

She was a local star, a famous beauty, fallen on hard times, and it was their way of taking care of their own.

Summer days in Harlem were filled with games and laughter, friendly firemen uncapping fire hydrants to give respite from the blazing sun, kids collecting bottles to save money for ice cream or movies.

Ordinarily, Benny would have passed the time with his friends, but today, he found himself keeping away from them, finding quiet places to sit, staring at the sky.

Something was wrong with his eyes. When people walked by, he could see ghosts trailing behind them . . . and extending in front of them, which was even creepier. Sometimes he would look at a group of people, and they were all like a train of souls, extended forward and back. He didn't know what was happening and just before he panicked, the effect stopped.

Twice, he heard auto horns before the horns blew. Once, he stepped aside on the street before a pie fell from a second-story kitchen ledge. And then, walking down the street, he bumped into a rack of clothing that had yet to be pushed out onto the sidewalk.

Benny stood, shivering, watching the cars, and the people pass him, seeing each of them not just as they were, but as they would be in a few more seconds, as if motion picture images were overlapping drastically.

In a movie theater, the effect might have been comical.

Here, and now, it was terrifying. He ran home, curled up on the couch, and slept until dark.

Dreaming of stars.

Benny sat on the stoop, looking up at the sky. What was it about those stars? He had never paid them such attention before. Had he just never noticed how beautiful they were?

"Benny!" he heard her before he saw her. Benny's heart raced when he caught a glimpse of Ardelia coming down the street. She was, to him, one of the most beautiful women in the world. Despite her fatigue, and he knew that she had just finished working a twelve-hour day, she still moved with a dancer's grace.

"Benny." Her face lit up at the sight of him. She bent down and kissed his forehead. "Did you have a good day?"

"Great, Ardelia." He wanted to tell her about the stars, but couldn't quite. Couldn't bring himself to go into that part of it. Not quite yet. So he told her more about the fair, and the Futurama, and the train ride, and the crowds, and about that moment in the ride when Jenny had touched his hand.

She smiled, hoisting her tired weight up the steps. He held the door for her. "Well," she said. "You never know. You may have something there, yet. But she has . . . a certain reputation, you know. Be careful."

"I will," Benny said. The hallway inside glowed

with a bare light bulb, the stair rug was threadbare, and the stairs creaked under their feet.

"Yes. Don't you go crossing that Willie. He's got a bad temper, I hear." She turned the key to let them into their apartment, then stopped, trembling with excitement.

"But I have some good news," she whispered. "On the way home, I looked in the mirror, and my reflection didn't quite look like me. I looked younger."

He helped her off with her coat.

"Ardelia," he said. "You're getting younger every day."

She shushed him and continued. "No, really. And you know what it says in Madame French's book, don't you?"

He winced. "No—what?"

"It says that reflections are a key to hitting the number." She sighed, straightened, letting her spine work some of the crackles out, and then went to her bookshelf, running her finger across the contents for a shelf before finding the one she wanted.

"Here . . ." she made her way quickly through the book, until she came to the reference she wanted.

He knew what Madame French's book was, of course. Most Harlemites did—French, or one of the innumerable other numerical prophets who claimed to help you hit the daily number based upon signs in dreams, or pig entrails, or cloud formations, or reflections, or the number of hairs on your comb.

Madame French was one of the very best. He had

watched his aunt attending one of her revival meet-
ings, held down at the old Showcase Theater, and had
to admit that French, garbed in her voluminous robes
and waving her hands theatrically over the sea of dark
faces watching her worshipfully, put on a very good
show indeed.

But he resented it that his aunt's substance continued to be drained, day after day, year after year, even
when the old fraud was working her magic on some
distant crowd. It felt wrong, but there was little or
nothing that he could do for it.

"Here it is," Ardelia said, excitedly. She thrust the
book under his nose, her finger marking out the
pertinent entry.

"When in a dream, or in real life, and a REFLEC-
TION appears to you, and the REFLECTION is
different from your own age, younger, the number is
673. Older, the number is 782. Add or subtract your
age from these numbers, of course, depending on the
color of your morning urine as described on page . . ."

"Oh, Ardelia," he groaned, throwing the book
down. "Can't you see what this is? That it's just a
bunch of crap?" A copy of the *Times* was laying on the
stand by the couch, and he flipped to the stock page.
There, at the top of the page, were the closing totals,
the last three numbers of which formed the daily
Number. He felt furious. "I could just make up a
number at random—," he said, but then, staring at it,
he stopped.

"I suppose that you could do better," she said.

"No—," but his vision had begun to blur, the

numbers dancing and jittering before his eyes, and the edges of the page seemed to multiply, as if he held not just today's paper, but yesterday's, and . . .

(Tomorrow's)

The voice was tiny inside him, but insistent. And he was surprised to hear it.

(Yes) it said again, and he closed his eyes, and he saw something, saw the Orb, the glowing hourglass of the Orb, and he was stumbling back, and he crashed against the wall, drawing thumping protestations from the couple on the far side.

When he opened them again, his Aunt was staring at him with concern. "Benny?" she said. "Are you all right?" Her face was filled with alarm and . . . and something else. But what?

He waved her away. "Yeah," he said. "Sure, I'm all right."

"It's just . . ."

There was something about her voice that made him stop. "Just what?" he asked.

"It's just that you never offered me a number before."

"What?" He knew what she was saying, but had a problem dealing with it—

(Yes)

"You said the number Four Sixty Two. Were you teasing me? Were you kidding, dear?"

"No," he said weakly. And he didn't know how he knew that, or why he had said it.

Only that he was as certain of it as he was of anything in his life. He looked at her, and nodded, afraid of the voices in his head.

If he was really certain, really *that* certain, shouldn't he tell her to bet more than her usual pennies? How much?

(Don't be greedy)

the voices said. And he knew that it would be wise to listen to them. Knew that they meant him no harm.

"Remember the money you were saving up to buy me a suit?" he said. He hardly knew what he was saying, knowing only that this was the right thing to say. "Take that whole twenty dollars."

"Twenty dollars?" she said. "Benny? Are you well?"

He smiled. "Never been better."

CHAPTER
17

"BENNY!" his Aunt was running, her dress hiked up with one hand, her feet slapping against the pavement, almost flying with her excitement.

Benny was sitting on the tenement stoop with a few of the regulars. Little Cass was there, and his gangling buddy Rike, and puff-eared Swoop, and the rest of the gang. The sun was setting and the long shadows were stretching across the street, but this was a good time, a time for gathering on the stoops, for shooting the breeze, bragging, talkin' trash.

This might be a time for talking about the latest ball game, or title bout. A time for talking about girls—or, if there were none about, for bragging about nonexistent conquests. In some ways, these gatherings were the centerpiece of the entire day—everything else just revolved around them. It was a ritual he had enjoyed since childhood.

So when they all turned their heads and saw Benny's Aunt Ardelia, her face lit up like a Christmas tree, there was much good-natured laughter and speculation about what might have been the occasion for such intense exercise.

They found out shortly. She looked at him with an expression of wonder in her eyes. "I . . . you . . ."

"What?"

Her wonder was mixed with something like sheepish guilt. "When you told me about the number, I didn't quite believe you. I thought that you were pulling my leg," she said. "So I didn't bet the whole twenty dollars."

He groaned. "How much, then?"

She looked at the ground. "Oh, Benny, forgive me. I only bet a dollar."

He closed his eyes hard, and saw the orb flashing and flashing around behind his eyes, and heard something that was almost like a kind of electric laughter. Six hundred dollars. That was enough to get them out of debt. Back rent and then some! That was enough to get a little ahead. But it could have been a hundred and twenty thousand!

He felt her hand on his arm. "Benny?" she said. Neither of them noticed that the stoop seemed to have gone quiet. Nobody said a word. "Benny?" she said again. "You can do it again, can't you Benny?"

He gulped, and backed up from them. He looked around. Every eye was on him and there was something in their eyes, a mixture of greed and wonderment. All except for Cass, who watched him with her lips pursed.

143

"Yeah, man—" Rike said. "Can you hit that number for me, too?"

"What's the number for tomorrow?" Swoop said. And gripped at him with cold fingers.

"I don't know. I don't know!" Benny tore himself away, and ran, as fast as he could, away from their clamor.

There was a place that Benny Russell could usually count on to find peace. It was up on the rooftop above the apartment he shared with his aunt, and he was leaning against one of the ventilator ducts when Cass found him. He sat with his knees drawn up against his chest, breathing hard, and eyes shut hard, trying to find the Orb behind his lids. Nothing.

He heard her footsteps in the silence behind his eyes, and glanced up at her. She seemed a little tentative, but smiled.

"They're all talking about your Aunt," she said. "Good timing, you know?"

"I guess we won't be sleeping in the street, after all," he said.

"All up and down the avenue," she said. "Willie Hawkins and Jenny came by, and you should have seen her eyes light up."

"They did?" Suddenly all of the fear, all of the doubt and insecurity seemed to vanish.

She just looked at him, and shook her head. She sat down beside him. "You're not as smart as you think you are," she said.

"None of us are."

"I mean, you're pretty smart, but you're not real smart about people. You don't see what I see."

"And what's that?"

"Oh . . . that you're good enough for Jenny when she wants to study, or when she thinks you might make her some money. But she's in love with Willie. You don't want a girl like her."

He looked at Cass, and just smiled to himself. He didn't tell her what he had seen.

He had closed his eyes, thinking of Jenny, wondering what this new and sudden gift might conceivably bring to his life, and had been blessed with a sudden image of Jenny kissing him, holding him on a rooftop, gripping him so intensely that even through a mere vision, he could feel the heat. The Orb had whispered to him: *"Don't be greedy."*

And he had allowed the vision to lapse.

Cass looked at him. There was something in her fourteen-year-old eyes that he hadn't quite let himself see before. Just a moment of it. And he realized that Jenny had practiced a kind of prognostication of her own. And that Cass, for all of her boyish ways, was in love with him, and he had never quite let himself see it.

No, he wasn't really very smart, at all.

He reached out, and brushed her face with the back of his hand. "I'll just have to do the best I can," he said. "That's all that any of us can do."

"Can you really pick the number?" she asked. He noticed that there was no second question behind that. No *"and will you pick one for me?"* There was just a general curiosity. She had been there at the fair. She might be willing to believe.

"I don't know what you'd call it," he said. "I got something at the fair. It's weak, but sometimes it gets a little stronger. The Orb did something to me."

She squatted there, watching him, without judgment in her sweet little brown eyes. And finally, she said: "Then you'd better go back."

Benny was a hero the next day, and the day after. He and his aunt were local celebrities—they had hit the number, and for six hundred dollars! That was big, big news around here. If her bosses had thought Eva capable of rigging the number (as "Dutch" Shultz had been rumored to do) they would have looked at her askance. As it was, there was a flurry of curiosity, and she paid off her debts, bought herself a new dress, and Benny that new suit, and then pestered him, every moment, about when he was going to give her another number.

And she wasn't the only one. It seemed that everyone along the street knew that his Aunt had hit the number, and that he had given it to her after falling into some kind of spell.

He had money for movies—Ardelia made sure of that, and they saw Republic chapter plays and cowboy movies, and bought ice cream, and once went all the way out to Coney Island.

Several times during those days, he thought that he caught Jenny peering at him, but although she sometimes cruised by, or he saw her laughing as she walked along with Willie Hawkins, or once, when he went to a youth baseball game, and watched the local team pound the starch out of a colored team from Bed-Sty, he saw Jenny in the stands. She wore a peach dress that clung to her like sin, and she was eating an ice cream cone. She turned to look at him, licking lazily at that cone with an idly speculative expression, he knew that he was just going to burst.

The celebrity faded. A number had been hit, but numbers were hit every day. When nothing more exciting happened, life along 127th drifted back to normal.

And there it might have stayed, except that a week later, he ran into Jenny in the Sweet Temptations ice cream shop.

She sat in a booth with Willie, who was roaring with laughter and regaling them with his latest exploits—these in the boxing ring when he had thrashed some local challenger. Benny sat at the counter by himself, sipping at a coke.

He heard Willie laugh and then say: "Well, I have to get to practice. Team can't make it without me!" Then he slid his big body out of the booth and hurried out the door, stopping only long enough to slap Benny on the shoulder.

"Hey Benny!" he said. "Got any predictions about the game tonight? Or maybe what I'm going to be doing after."

He roared uproariously and lewdly, glancing back at Jenny. She dimpled and turned her face away. The other boys chuckled heartily.

Embarrassed for her, Benny squeezed his eyes shut and . . .

And this time, there was something in the darkness. It spun and hummed there behind his closed lids, glowing, and it spoke to him. For almost ten seconds he listened.

Then he opened his eyes and said: "Yeah, Willie. I know what's going to happen in the game. You're going to lose. Worse, you're going to twist your ankle pretty bad, and the only thing you're going to do tonight is soak it."

The entire ice cream shop went dead quiet. Willie blinked hard, and leaned close. "What did you say?"

"I think you heard me," Benny said calmly. "I said you're going to lose, and get hurt. And be too busy limping to chase after Jenny."

Willie got just a little closer to Benny, and then blinked again, and backed away.

"Come on, man!" Willie's friends said, pulling him back away. Willie was still looking at Benny, and Benny saw something in the larger boy's eyes that he had never seen before.

Fear.

The sound of Willie's car peeling away from the curb was music to his ears. He sighed deeply, and let himself relax. He hardly realized it when Jenny slid onto the stool next to him.

"Ooh," she said. "You really zinged him with that one."

"Wasn't what I was trying to do," he said. She was drenched in some kind of mind-spinning perfume, something almost insanely intoxicating. He wanted to faint, or die, or throw her over his shoulder and run.

"I heard about the number," she said. "You know, I

believe that sometimes people can see things, you know?" She shivered, and the action animated her entire body. "You know? A man who can do things like that is a lot of man. I could be interested in him."

She leaned a little closer, and before he realized what had happened, deposited a kiss on the corner of his mouth. "Bye," she said, and sashayed out of the shop.

His heart roared, and the blood sang *hallelujah* in his ears. He didn't know what to do. He was supposed to buy some shoes, but there was something else calling to him now, and he wasn't certain he could resist.

He left a nickel on the counter, and made his way to the train station.

SHUFFLE

CHAPTER
18

1953

BENNY WASN'T completely certain how he made it home. He switched trains automatically, not really paying attention to the stops. He walked as if he had lead weights attached to his feet. God help him, that was exactly how it felt.

He managed to make it back across 138th Street without being run over, or exploding with grief and anger and fear and simply striking down some innocent passerby. Anyone. Just to have a chance to take the darkness out of himself and put it somewhere else. Anywhere else. Just not in his own heart. It was so crowded in there. He had collected so much darkness in there over the years, there seemed no room left for love.

He climbed the stairs to his room and fit the key to the door. Forty dollars a month. That was what it took him to keep a roof over his head. He needed every penny from whatever source. And when it came right down to it, wasn't the preservation of life and basic human needs important? Wasn't that victory of a kind? So even if he ignored his muse just a bit, channeled his artistic drive into the fields of commercial necessity, was that so bad?

Comforted by his lies, Benny drifted from exhausted wakefulness to an uneasy sleep, and there found surcease of sorrow.

He woke in the morning feeling even less rested, if that was possible. Benny rolled out of bed, staring at his hands, which shook. He needed food, and coffee, and even more than that, he needed a friendly face.

A quick shower washed his dark, sticky dreams down the drain. He brushed his teeth without enthusiasm. No matter how he scrubbed, it felt as if a thin film remained. No efforts, however sincere, could completely wash away the muck.

His dreams had been shallow and restless, shifting between scenes without respect for narrative flow (and here Benny realized, ironically, that he truly was as slave to the muse. Even in dream, he couldn't just let his mind wander where it would. Even in dream, he bowed to the compulsion to exert some creative control.)

He could feel the headache building up behind his ears again, and along with that, something whispered to him, something that grew stronger with every breath. Some revelation was tumbling up from the depths of his unconscious, something . . .

Something that would help him to make sense of his life?

That was a consummation to be devoutly wished. Why couldn't he be happy with the life that he had been given? Why couldn't he be happy moving through the world as other men did, accepting the world around them? There was peace, there was contentment in such bliss. And if there were times when he thought that such peace was bought at the price of blindness, he also knew that it was too easy to criticize those who had chosen the more well-trodden path.

He looked about himself, at the place in which he lived. He had his father's piano, and a table, and a typewriter. And, of course, a bed on which he usually slept alone. He was thirty years old, and as his father would have said, "you ain't gonna be twenty-nine next year, boy."

Benny's aunt had feared for her dreamer nephew. It wasn't just Cassie who thought that he was wasting his time. But his aunt had been afraid for another reason: she feared that he was simply trying to follow in his father's footsteps. His father had written songs, and played them with magical fingers on that old piano. And followed his dream even when his dream threatened to lead his family into the poorhouse. And if that dream had ultimately broken him, costing "Fox" his wife, and his son, at least he had followed it, right down the line. And how many people in this world could say that they had done such a thing?

So if he was in some way following the path that his father had marked out for him, he supposed that there were worse and less honest things that he could do with his life.

But what about Cassie? Wasn't it unfair to her? Wasn't it some kind of self-indulgent, egotistical dishonesty to continue their relationship? When it came right down to it, he knew that he was willing to starve for his art, for his writing, for the precious words placed on paper. But was he really willing to ask *Cassie* to starve for his art?

When it came down to it, wouldn't he be happy to live by himself, even in such conditions as this, and work, and work, and continue to strive, if he managed to put some of his dreams onto paper? What a miracle if some of them were even published, and he would know that someone out there somewhere knew that he had lived, that he had striven, and fought, and made his mark?

But that was what a man did. A man did things, a man changed things. Men had to *do*. Women could simply *be*. And simple being for a woman meant a family. And stability. And marriage. Things that he could not offer her, unless he succeeded.

Or gave up his dream.

He was trembling again, and knew it. Outside the window of his apartment, there were cars, and the clamor of conversations and a world that moved from day to day, and deed to deed, and people who had made their peace with the world that was. Perhaps making that peace was the key to opening one's heart, finding contentment.

As he could not.

As Cassie could not, so long as she loved him.

Something had to change, something had to shift. He wasn't sure that he was the immovable object he had often imagined himself to be. There was the muse. And there was Cassie and all that she represented. Both were irresistible forces, before which he was as a straw in the wind.

What will you do? What will you choose?

"Why me?" he asked aloud. And there was no answer. Why couldn't he just have an ordinary life? Why him? And there were no answers from the room, or the walls, or anyone or anything. No answers at all.

Eva's Kitchen was, surprisingly, almost empty. He was glad of it, though—right now he had no taste for a crowd, or a boisterous Willie bragging about the game, or even little Jimmy pulling one of his endless scams. Right now he just wanted to sip his coffee and be left alone.

Then his solitude was ruptured. Jimmy bounced through the door and sat beside him, casually spinning himself around on the stool as Cassie refilled Benny's cup. With perfect—perfectly bad—timing, she said, "I'm sorry they didn't buy your story, baby. Really I am."

Jimmy smiled grimly, one of those smiles that invite the recipient to share in one of the great and dark secrets of the world. "I told you," he said. "I knew you were wasting your time." He shook his head, but it wasn't just disgust. There was something just a little bit wistful about it. "Colored captain . . . the only reason they'll ever let us in space is if they need someone to shine their shoes. Ain't that right, Cassie?"

"I don't know," she said, "and to be honest, I don't much care what happens a hundred years from now. It's today that matters."

Benny listened to them, wondering if they understood how much their dialogue mirrored his own internal conversations. It wasn't what he needed. What he needed now was someone to say: *believe in yourself, Benny! There is hope, keep going—*

But there wasn't anyone, had never really been, and he knew that he was going to have to pull himself out of the depression, or let these people—his friends— turn him into something that they would feel comfortable with. And who would he be then?

Jimmy was warmed up, and progressed well into his rap. "Well I got news for you . . . today or a hundred years from now don't make a bit of difference . . . as far as they're concerned, we'll always be niggers."

Benny sighed, hard. "Things are going to change." He said. What he didn't say to them, but did to himself was: *They have to.*

Jimmy wasn't buying it for a second. "Yeah, you just keep telling yourself that." Jimmy pushed himself off the stool and walked away.

Benny closed his eyes. *Maybe if I wish really hard, and really strong, I'll open my eyes and be far away from here. Maybe I can just step into that world in my imagination. And Cassie will be Kasidy Yates, and Jimmy will be Jake Sisko, and I'll be Benjamin Sisko, captain of* Deep Space Nine, *a man respected and loved by not merely members of all the human race, but a hundred other species as well. Or feared and hated and loathed. Anything. But if they love me, it's because of the fact that I'm me. Or if they hate me, it's because I'm me. Or maybe because I'm a human being. Not because my ancestors came from a tropical continent. Not because my skin is dark. Please not because of that. If I have any more of that, any more at all, I could begin to hate myself, and that would be the same as letting them win.*

Cassie's light touch upon his hand pulled him back to reality. Her face was so filled with compassion that it was impossible for him to take offense at what he knew she was about to say. "Maybe this is happening for a reason."

"You mean . . . maybe this is God's way of telling me to quit writing and go into the restaurant business?"

He meant it facetiously, but Cassie met him head on. "Hey," she said. "It's possible."

Then she leaned closer and, in full view of the others in the restaurant, kissed him on the lips. That was the first time that she had ever done that. "Baby," she said, "I know we could make this work for us. We could be happy here."

Benny shook his head slowly, and a bit miserably. "It's not that simple."

"Yes," Cassie said, with a wisdom as old as the sea. "It is. Or it could be, if you let it."

Benny looked deeply into her eyes, desperately wishing he could accept what she was saying. What was so wrong with that? What was so awful about living a simple, normal life with a woman who adored him? In most of human history, had people ever possessed, or even *aspired* to more than that? What was wrong with him, and was it too late to be able to fix it?

Suddenly, and with perverse timing, a hand dropped onto Benny's shoulder.

"Hey," a *too*-familiar voice said jovially. "Hear the game last night?"

Benny turned, sighing, knowing what he would see, knowing that Willie would be standing there in his finery, a constant and painful reminder of the success which had always eluded him. And—

But it wasn't Willie. Instead he saw the giant Klingon, Worf, in full battle regalia, his eyes blazing from beneath scarred brows, eyes that had seen a thousand battles, which had exalted in the death of countless foes, that welcomed the possibility of death as a test of his own mettle.

What was it that Klingon Worf said, that was virtually the credo by which he lived?

"Today is a good day to die—"?

Benny hadn't realized how far he had jumped back away from this apparition. His heart raced, thundered. What in the hell was going on—

Worf (Willie?) looked at him with an expression of concern. "Hey," he said, in Willie's voice, "I didn't mean to frighten you."

Benny closed his eyes and rubbed his forehead, as if trying to massage his frontal lobes. In the darkness, something red pulsed. It was an irregular shape, but in the moments when it began to coalesce, it looked a bit like an hourglass.

When he opened his eyes again, Worf had become Willie again. Willie reached over, trying to help Benny back to his seat. "You don't look so good," Willie said. There was no teasing now, nothing but concern, and Benny gained another insight into Willie.

Willie really liked him. Really . . . Why? Maybe, just maybe because every time Willie stepped up to bat, a million people were watching and listening. Maybe because every time he did, he put everything he had, everything he *was* at stake, and that gamble was enough to break most people. Most people just wanted comfort, and a little piece of the world where they could settle in and find respite. Very few wanted to put their butt on the line every day.

Willie was . . . a warrior. Yes, that was it. He was one of the ones who took a risk. Willie *had* to believe that every day, every time he stepped up, might be a good day to die. It was to the Willies of the world that the rewards belonged. It had always been like that, and always would. And Willie, regardless of whether he could show it or not, admired Benny's willingness to sacrifice for his dream.

Benny, like Willie, bet everything every time he stepped up to the plate. In a quieter, smaller way, perhaps, but they were both kamikazes.

"I'm fine," Benny said.

"Want to lie down in the back?" Cassie asked.

"I just need some air," Benny assured them.

Cassie looked dubious. "We still on for tonight?"

He nodded, the vision, and its sudden revelation, retreating into the back of his mind. "I'll pick you up around ten."

Benny managed to force his mouth into a smile that he didn't really feel, then rose and headed for the door.

Willie and Cassie watched him leave. As soon as the door closed behind him, Willie leaned over the counter. "So," he asked. "What are you doing until ten?" He smiled brilliantly.

She leaned close, and lowered her voice to a conspiratorial hush. "Whatever it is," she said, "I'm not doing it with you."

He laughed and winked at her, completely unfazed as she turned away and returned to her work.

Benny walked aimlessly down the street, increasingly lost in his own world. He fought to make sense of his hallucination.

This was becoming frightening. He had always had the ability to lose himself in the world of his imagination. It had been his salvation throughout his childhood, an ability that had accelerated after . . . that summer. But it had always been under control, had never produced visions as stark as these, almost as if some barrier between his imagination and reality had begun to fray. If that was true, then . . . he wasn't certain what he could do. Or who, indeed, he was.

If you can't trust your mind, when your mind is the only thing which has protected you during a long and sometimes painful life, then what do you do?

"Hello, Brother Benny," the Preacher said.

Benny was startled out of his reverie, and turned to see the familiar black-suited figure of the Preacher emerging from the shadowed mouth of an alley. "You again?" he said.

The Preacher spread his arms. "The Good Book says: 'Let us run with perseverance the race marked out for us.' Follow the path of righteousness and you shall be righteous in the eyes of the Prophets."

Benny wasn't quite tracking. "I don't understand," he said. "What do you want from me?"

The Preacher's eyes burned. "To follow in your path. The path of the Prophets. Walk with the Prophets, Brother Benny. Show us the way."

The words added to his confusion rather than subtracting from it. "What way? I don't know what you're talking about."

Benny turned away from the Preacher and continued walking down the sidewalk. The Preacher stayed where he was, but called out to him: "Write the words, Brother Benny. The words that will lead us out of the darkness—that will lead us to righteousness."

Benny kept walking, faster and faster—but the Preacher's words kept racing after him. He tried to outpace them, but they kept floating after him, catching up with him, and there was no place to hide.

Write the words, Brother Benny. Write the words.

Benny ran, the sound of his feet slapping against the sidewalk, the sound of his own breathing in his lungs, the thunder of his heart drowning out the words reverberating in his mind.

He ran up the stairs to his apartment, fumbling the

door open and then quickly shutting it behind him. He stopped to catch his breath.

It took a few minutes for his breathing to slow, for his heartbeat to slow. His vision blurred when he walked through the door, began to clear, and finally he was able to orient.

Walk with the Prophets, Brother Benny. Show us the way.

Hell. Who could he show anything to? Hell, he couldn't even show himself anything. He should give the whole thing off. He should grab that damned typewriter and—

He looked at it, and it sat there, a solid metal block, black and impenetrable, calling to him and laughing at him at the exact same time.

He walked to it, and lay his fingers on it, feeling the tidal force that seemed to project from it, from the metal itself. It flowed from his heart, from his mind, creating a current that was like putting lightning on the page. He waited to feel it, and felt nothing, nothing but the typewriter. Damnably silent, it laughed at him in its stolid metallic way.

He picked it up, surprised by how light it felt in his hands. He could do it. Just throw it through the window, send the damned thing hurtling out of the window down into the street below. He could do it, and never look back, be done with it, be through with the pain and the fear and the disappointment. Get on with his life, marry Cassie . . .

But then he caught a glimpse of himself in the window, a glimpse of his own image. And he didn't look like Benny Russell. He was Benjamin Sisko, and what he held over his head wasn't a typewriter, it was something that was vaguely hourglass shaped, something that glowed in his hands as if consumed by an internal flame. He looked into the face of the man in the reflection, and knew that somehow, this man was more than just a part of his imagination. Knew that the image floating there would still be there no matter how hard he blinked. That in fact the only way he could force the image to dissipate was if he stopped, if he gave up something that it was not his to abandon.

He was trapped, and didn't know why or how, knew only that he lowered the typewriter back to the desk, and began to write.

CHAPTER
19

IT WAS NIGHTTIME in Harlem. The cars outside still rolled but now there was a special rhythm to the blare of their horns. The inhabitants seemed to sense that there was freedom in the night. And as they emerged in their night finery, and the streetlights glowed to life, there was a shift in mood, a sense that the nights of New York belonged to them in a way that the days could not.

Benny lay stretched across his typewriter, asleep. Papers were scattered all about the table, crumpled into balls, some stacked in a ragged pile.

His eyes opened groggily as the radio clicked on next to him, and began to play some soft, easy jazz. After another few moments, the smoothness of a woman's hand came to rest on his shoulder, and began rubbing his back.

He grumbled, and moved just slightly, purring to

respond to her touch. "Hey, baby," Cassie said. "You forgot all about our date."

He fought his way up to full wakefulness. Once again, it seemed his dreams had exhausted him. "Date?" he said. "Oh, yeah—that's right. I'm sorry. I was working . . ."

Cassie peered over his shoulder, scanning the paper in his typewriter. Benny used the few moments' respite to work himself back to some kind of decent state of wakefulness, finally remembering completely where he was, and what he had been doing before he fell asleep.

"Ben Sisko?" she asked. "Isn't that your colored captain?"

He nodded assent.

"Why are you writing another one of those stories? You couldn't sell the last one. What makes you think that this one will be any different?"

Benny lowered his eyes, and found the strength within himself to tell the truth. "It probably won't be. Doesn't matter."

Today is a good day to die . . .

"It's just what I've got to do," he said.

Cassie took his face in her hands, and finally leaned forward and kissed him very gently. "Right now, what you've got to do is eat." She held up a paper bag.

"What's that?"

She smiled shyly. "I thought that it might save some time if we didn't have to go out for dinner."

Suddenly, a fascinating portion of his fatigue seemed to lift from his shoulders. "And what were you thinking we could do with the extra time?"

164

"It's a little after midnight. I should be in bed soon," she said. He rose, tried to take her in his arms. She held her fingertips out, pushing him back just a little. Just enough. "But first—"

"First?" he asked, all exhaustion forgotten now.

She stepped into his arms, and swayed against him slowly. "What do you say we take one spin around the dance floor."

He closed his eyes and held her close, allowing the pleasure of the moment to distract him from the dreams and the fears.

"Feels good, doesn't it?" Cassie said.

"I could stay like this forever," he murmured.

Cassie raised her head from his shoulder. Benny looked down at her and her eyes were as deep as the oceans, waiting for him to accept, to simply let it be between them.

Then—

SHUFFLE

CHAPTER
20

BENNY WAS HOLDING CASSIE. Only it wasn't Cassie, it was Kasidy Yates. He was in Sisko's living quarters, wearing Sisko's clothes.

"I could dance like this forever," Benny/Sisko heard himself say.

"Me, too," Kasidy said. "It's times like these that I wish we'd never heard of the Dominion."

Benny stopped, staring, looking around. Where in the world was he? How did he get here? This was no place he had ever been—and yet it was. That window, with its view out onto a sky filled with impossibly bright stars. Where was he?

But he never stopped dancing. "The Dominion?" he asked.

SHUFFLE

CHAPTER
21

"WHAT DO YOU MEAN?" Cassie said. She stared up into Benny's face, confused by his confusion. "You said something about the Dominion."

Benny was still looking around, trying to regain his bearing. His mouth was slightly open. Finally, his gaze met Cassie's and—

SHUFFLE

CHAPTER
22

THE STARS WERE pinpoints in black velvet suspended over the furnace that birthed the universe.

"What is it?" Kasidy Yates asked the man in her arms. "What is it, Ben? What's wrong?"

Benny Russell gazed out at the stellar display. Without warning, there was a flash of light, a swirl of incandescence as the Bajoran wormhole opened, a churning hole through the fabric of reality.

He gazed at it, lost in wonder as a freighter appeared, a visitor from far light-years, and headed toward the station. The funnel of light closed behind it.

"I . . . I don't know," Benny said as sincerely as he had ever said anything in his life. "I think I'm losing my mind."

SHUFFLE

CHAPTER
23

"WHY?" CASSIE ASKED Benny as they danced in his apartment. "What's wrong?"

Benny held her slightly away from him, as if afraid that he might somehow infect her. "I'm starting to see things. Things from my story . . . it's as if I'm becoming Captain Sisko."

Benny broke off the dance and slumped onto the couch, holding his head in his hands.

Cassie came to him and put her arm around his shoulders. "Baby," she said. "You need to get some rest."

She sat next to him on the couch and wrapped her arms around him. "It's all right baby. I'm here. Just take it easy . . . I'm with you."

She cradled Benny in her arms, rocking him back and forth, gazing out the window as if, in that moment, she was as confused as he.

"I'm with you," she said again, as if it was all she could say, all she needed to say.

And perhaps she was right.

SHUFFLE

CHAPTER
24

1940

IT SEEMED TO TAKE forever for Benny Russell to reach Flushing Meadow. The crowds were a little lighter this time—in fact, he heard it rumored that the fair's promoters were worried that it wouldn't make its money back. He had a hard time believing that, seeing all of the many people and the vast throngs—how could anyone lose money? And yet that was what they said. Oh well.

For him, he was happy to pay his seventy-five cents and be admitted back on the promenade, making his way once again to the Hall of Nations, that humble structure in the shadow of the Perisphere.

There were fewer Hall of Nations visitors this time, as well. Many of them seemed ethnic types—Serbs, Slavs, Hispanics—people who had come to the exhibit primarily out of loyalty to the homelands they had left far behind in all but heart. Many of the stalls were deserted, but the one from the Mali Republic had four people sitting there, listening to the small dark man named Ajabwe talk about deals made with creatures from another world, and leaders, and dreams. They listened politely, filed past the exhibit, and then went on their way. One of them was an unusually tall and somewhat gangly Negro man. He wore the black cloth of a preacher, and as he rose Benny was certain that he had seen him before, holding forth on biblical topics on street corners all over Harlem.

As he filed past the gemstone, he reached his hand out—not to touch but to bask in its radiance. He tilted his head back, mouth open, eyes squeezed shut, as if receiving some ecstatic vision. Then he nodded, almost as if concluding a satisfactory conversation with a wise friend, and went on his way.

As the Preacher passed the curtain concealing Benny he paused, and cocked his head, listening to sounds Benny couldn't detect. He stopped for so long that Benny was certain that the Preacher somehow knew he was there, and was about to flee. Then, a secretive smile on his face, the older man continued on, and was gone.

Ajabwe waited, and scanned the room, not spotting Benny behind the curtain. He shifted from foot to foot, and then finally drew the curtain across his exhibit, and headed back toward a lavatory that Benny had spotted near the entrance.

Almost immediately, Benny left his place of hiding, and scampered across to the curtained alcove. He knew that he wasn't supposed to be here, but it seemed to call to him. And it was increasingly difficult to resist the call. With each step, he felt it pulling, with each step it seemed to speak to him of a world beyond this one, and it frightened him.

He understood the world he lived in, knew the stoops and streets of Harlem. He knew that in time he would take his place, would run numbers, make book—or perhaps he would finally find the spark of magic in his piano-playing, and maybe be able to make a living there.

But for the most part, he could feel that he was . . . well, *waiting* for something. That there was some fate for him, some destiny for a skinny little Negro boy, something that he could not, as yet, dream of.

It was impossible to believe that this thing, whatever it was, could hold any answers for him. And yet . . . and yet . . .

He knew that there was a part of him that believed just that.

Just that.

He brushed the curtain aside, and gazed at it.

Looked at this closely, the object seemed more as if it had been made out of glass. It didn't hum. It didn't glow, and he felt foolish at first to have squandered his hard-earned money, to have thought that there could possibly be anything unusual or great about this odd thing.

But . . .

He reached out to touch it—

SHUFFLE

CHAPTER
25

BENNY GASPED. It seemed that he was standing in the middle of a pool of water, only he was somehow sideways to the surface, and it reflected his face. There was more than one of him, and in fact, at this moment there seemed to be an infinite string of Bennys. One was dressed in the kind of twenties hipster clothes he had seen in his father's closet, and he wondered at that. And there was one dressed in a very conservative suit—better than anything Benny owned. But this Benny's head was bowed, his face heavily lined, as if the weight of the world hung on his bony shoulders. Strangely, he intuited that this Benny, this past Benny, was no older than he. And there was a Benny before that. A barefoot Benny wearing the clothes of a farmer. And then, before that, there was a Benny who wore the chains of a slave.

His heart was thumping so fast that he thought it

174

would burst out of his chest. He wanted to scream, but no words would emerge from his throat.

Several Bennys were slaves. One wore the mark of the lash over his naked, muscular chest. One had had an eye burned out. Some seemed healthy and fit, but their faces were hooded, guarded, and the flame of awareness was almost extinguished.

And he saw flashes of their lives—hard work, generations of thankless labor, generations who had suffered long years of deprivation in the service of men who considered them animals, who could buy or sell them, could force them to mate as they chose, could take their wives and children and sell them at their pleasure.

The sheer oppressive weight of it was almost more than he could bear. He could feel the pressure crushing him down, breaking him down so that there was almost no strength to push back with, nothing inside him to say *Yes! I am a human being, the same as you.*

He saw the cost of that, and felt what these men felt, knew that what they had endured was almost beyond his reckoning, and he cried out for relief, and release.

He saw an even earlier Benny, one who crossed the ocean in chains, one surrounded by filth and vomit, in brotherhood with the miserable chained creatures around him, stolen from their land and shipped to the other side of the world to toil in anguish. Benny, in some disconnected part of himself, realized that he had sagged to his knees, and if he could have broken the connection between himself and the gem, he would have.

But it went further still . . .

Further into pain, into shame, into degradation, until he thought that he could not bear even one more moment of this, until he was certain he would die—

Then suddenly, and quite unexpectedly, there was peace.

Benny was floating now, above another scene. It was not idyllic, no. It was a world of work, and sometimes danger. But he was tilling a field in a green land—hard work, but the cattle he herded were *his* cattle, and the fruit of his labors belonged to *him*. There were children—*he had children?*—and he realized that in this land, at seventeen, he was already a man, a young warrior, who had proven himself and taken a wife.

He watched her walk to him, bringing him a bowl of some kind of grain, mixed with sliced bananas. Her face was round and lovely, somehow different from the faces of Negro women in America. Her eyes were bright and filled with mischief, and on her head she wore a hat made of some kind of bright, folded cloth. Two small children were with her, and he understood that these were *his* children. The scene continued to play out, showing moments from this man's, this Benny's life. Walking to market. Harvesting. Celebrating. In what might have been moments, he experienced the totality of this Benny's existence. And then, on a day when the sun hid in shame behind treacherous clouds, he watched as men—black men—burst from behind bushes and captured this Benny, and his wife. His fleeing children were ignored.

He and his woman were shackled, and carried to

ships, to be handed to white men, who paid the black ones in guns.

Benny lay curled on the ground, sobbing. Black men had stolen him? It was for their power that he had lost his freedom, his lands, his woman, his children?

If this was true, then there was nothing but to hate all of humanity. There was no one, nothing to love in all the world. He was in a dark and lonely cave, and as far as he was concerned, could stay there for the rest of his life.

It was almost too painful to watch the earlier Bennys' lives unfold. These were men who worked, hunted, crafted, loved, fought and died as free men, never dreaming of the fate which lay ahead of them.

And what might they have thought, what might they have done if they had known that avaricious enemies would sail across the ocean to claim them, to haul them away?

Would they have thought themselves inferior? Would they have feared? Would they have thought themselves animals? Would they have hated, railed against the elements, cursed their gods?

Benny didn't know, because life for these men was untainted with the shadow of slavery, was without the slightest awareness of the tragedy to come.

They were unaware of their "inferiority," if that was what it was that made them vulnerable to the monsters from across the sea. They were too busy loving their children and wives, tilling their land, raising their cattle, fishing their seas.

Benny wept.

The line of eternal Bennys stretched further and further back, their days a blur, and all the same, ultimately . . .

Until one day . . .

A Benny, many generations back, stood casting his nets from the shore. He was older than many of the other Bennys, but beneath the beard it was clearly the same man, with a lean, muscular body, and the carriage of a king.

Lightning split the sky above him, and the clouds boiled with flame. Benny covered his face. He cowered as he watched the ocean turn crimson.

Then *something*—a streak of fire unlike any lightning he had ever seen, screamed down out of the sky and struck the water. Where it struck, the water churned and steamed.

Benny stood at the shore line, watching the display. Flame capered upon the waves, perhaps half a mile offshore, too far to swim. It was as terrifying as anything he had ever seen, but . . .

Something in the back of Benny's mind screamed at him.

There was some creature in pain out there, out beyond the surf, and without knowing what he was doing or entirely why he was doing it, Benny took his boat and began to paddle out through the surf. Something liquid flamed along the waves in little pools, and Benny was afraid that the boat would catch fire, but he maneuvered through the maze. As he came closer, he saw what seemed to be a big boat made of metal, something still incalescent and boiling the water around it.

The side of it opened, and a man—or something that looked vaguely like a man—crawled out, its skin searing where it touched the side of the vessel. Strapped to its back was a sack of some kind. It tried to make it to the water but strength failed it and it lay on one of the metal protrusions, the flames lapping at it terribly.

A voice—one which sounded *between* his ears rather than *in* them, screamed in agony.

Without understanding why, Benny dove from his boat, and swam in powerful strokes through the blazing ocean. Flame seared his hair, and he swallowed water as he dove to avoid burning. He was afraid, longed to turn back, but he kept hearing that voice in his head, kept hearing the call of a creature, different from him, but not so different that it could not feel pain, not fear death—crying for help.

He reached it, and burned his own arms pulling it down the metal wing. It opened its eyes and looked at him, and they were so soft and deep, so filled with pain and fear, and yet with a kind of peace that Benny would carry with him always.

He pulled the creature back to his canoe and began to paddle toward land.

By the time Benny got to the beach, the strange metal ship had vanished beneath the waves.

The man—if man it was, was barely breathing. His thin, fleshy lips pulled back from strange irregular teeth, its bloated abdomen sighed and bellowed as if it were trying to give birth. It clutched at Benny's hand, as if afraid to let him go. Again he met its eyes. And it spoke to him:

I come from far away, it said. *From a star called—*

(And here the star creature said something which made no sense. Benny, and then-Benny, interpreted it as a symbolic maze of distances and vectors, things which had to do with degrees of arc and gulfs light might cross over a span of years. And another part of Benny, one which was yet to be born, a future Benny said to him that the star the creature referred to was called Sirius.)

I was given a gift, one that I should have shared with my people. Instead, I fled with it, intending to sell it. I traded with the wrong . . .

(And here there was an image that Benny couldn't quite make out. Pirates? Thieves? Something dangerous, something deadly. Something that would search for what had eluded it.)

I escaped them, but they damaged my ship. They cannot trace me here, but they will come one day. They will find your world. They will take everything.

The little creature seemed to be expending its final strength: it shucked the backpack and handed it to Benny. He looked inside and nearly fainted.

It was like a gem, twice the size of his fists, narrow in the middle and broad at either end. It glittered as he held it.

I thank you for trying to save me, the little creature said. *My sins could not be escaped. This is yours now—yours and your children's.*

The little creature reached out and with one nail, cut a little scratch in Benny's hand. He tried to jerk back, but with sudden, surprising strength, it held his arm, and held the wound over the surface of the gem.

Shocked, frightened, and surprised, Benny was also amazed. Where his blood touched the surface of the gem, the fluid didn't slide off, but was rather *absorbed*. The gem turned yellow, and then red, and then the purest white he had ever seen. It seemed to sing to him.

It is yours now, the little creature said. *Use it well. Do not be greedy.*

And with that, it closed its eyes, and died.

Benny stood there on the beach, gazing out over the steaming, burning ocean, holding the gem in his hands. He knew that he would bury the little creature, and then travel the miles to his village, where tonight, at the joining fire, he would tell them of a gift brought from the stars.

SHUFFLE

CHAPTER
26

BENNY LAY ON the exhibition hall floor, near insanity by now. He was curled upon his side, gibbering, the visions more than his mind could bear. Because now they flashed *forward*, back through all of the generations, and to the slavery, and through those generations, and through emancipation, through those hard years, to the present—and then—

Oh, dear God, and then—

Into his future. There was a Benny who graduated college, and then another who amassed a fortune selling hair pomade. A Benny who wasted his life with drugs, followed by one who saved lives and sacrificed his own as a firefighter.

And there followed a string of Bennys who were dedicated to service, each in a more advanced and enlightened world. A Benny who lived to see a Negro President. A Benny—

God! This was the Twenty-first century!

Who saw men and women living on the moon, who saw the eradication of poverty and hunger on Earth, who saw man spreading out to the stars—

The stars.

And a Benny who was a leader of men, a maker of history, one who strode those stars, one who would become a legend—

And that was when he awoke, screaming.

Benny remembered bursting from the Hall of Nations, remembered men trying to stop him, remembered confusion, fear, too many worlds, too many Bennys exploding through his mind. Remembered being completely incapable of stopping the visions.

He felt feverish, and barely remembered finding his way back to the train station, barely recalled dropping in his money, or the ride back to Harlem.

All he could think of was the stars.

Somehow, he managed to make it back to the house he shared with his aunt. He was having a difficult time remembering what had happened, the fragmentary memories already melting away like night frost before the morning sun.

He saw no one that he knew along the way—or if he did, he didn't remember that he knew them, or that they might have called out to him, might have seen his zombie-like figure lurching its way through the streets.

He remembered crawling onto his couch. He recalled vivid, electric dreams of the past, and of the future, and of *otherwhen,* but couldn't remember what had *happened* in those dreams. And when he awoke at three in the morning, tossing on the couch, he was no longer certain that he had ever been out to the fair at all.

Was, in fact, no longer certain of anything.

And by the time he awoke in the morning, he remembered nothing except that he had gone to the fair and wandered, but until the day he died, he would not remember what he had done, or what he had seen.

"And you're telling me that this number will hit sometime this week?" the big man said. Benny nodded numbly.

Big Sid was the local numbers banker. He had run things for years, and was, although a relatively small fish in the overall structure of things, a big man in the neighborhood. His mother and aunt had gone to school with Big Sid, and Sid, a fat, rather unattractive boy even then (judging from pictures) had always coveted his aunt, and while mourning her declining fortunes on the one hand, secretly enjoyed the influence he had gained on the other.

He drummed his fingers. "And whatchu want me to do, boy?"

"Sometime in the next week," Benny said calmly, "this number is going to hit, and at six hundred to one, that's good odds even if it took six months to hit, isn't it?" Benny waited, watching the adding machine behind Big Sid's eyes clicking through its paces. After a few more seconds, it came up dollar signs. "But it's just a week. I can't call it closer than that. Then after it does, I want you to help me place some bets," he said. "I'll need you to do that."

Big Sid smiled and nodded. "Ardelia told me about that freak number you came up with. Got her a nice little pot of change. But you're right—if you do it again, we got us a little problem. At six hundred to one, it would be easier to kill your sorry black behind than pay you off, if the payoff is too high. We'll have to come up with something else."

Ardelia leaned forward. "But we can do it?"

"Ooh, yes." His little eyes gleamed greedily. "There are always ways."

He looked at Benny as if he wanted to eat him up utterly. "You just wait a couple days, and if you hit the number again, Big Sid, he's going to take good care of you. Best believe it."

Benny and Ardelia left the parlor, and he felt a small black cloud pulsing behind his eyes. *Don't be greedy,* it said.

"Benny?" she asked, studying him with concern. "Are you all right?"

He nodded. "I think I just need to be by myself for a while."

Ardelia looked almost panicked but she also realized that she couldn't dissuade him. "All right, but— you take care of yourself."

He waved her off and walked down to the youth center.

The kids there stared at him, and a couple of them started to walk away. He was wondering what the hell *that* was all about, when Cass approached him.

"Willie's ticked off big time," she said. "I think that you should lay low."

"Why?" he asked, his head still spinning.

"You said he was going to lose, and he lost. You said he was going to twist his ankle, and he did."

Benny almost giggled, but managed to repress it. "Then I guess you're right—I'd better go."

He had turned around and headed toward the door when a voice boomed out: "Where do you think you're going, punk?" The voice, beyond any doubt, was Willie. Worse, his entire coterie accompanied him.

Worse still, Jenny was there. She pulled at Willie's arm, tugging him back out toward the street. "Willie," she said, "don't do this."

"Little punk jinxed me," Willie said. "Put some kinda hoodoo into my head. How else you explain fouling out the way I did? Twisting my ankle chasing a damned grounder?"

He stalked toward Benny, and seemed to fill up the entire room. "I'm going to get you, Benny," he said. "Maybe not here today, but you'd better keep looking over your shoulder—"

Another voice came from behind them. "Wait a minute, boys—let's not have that." It was Cooley, wearing gray athletic sweats and resembling a stork even more than usual. "If there has to be a fight, let's have it right here, in the center, with some rules, all right?"

Benny thought that over. They could fight here, and he would get creamed, or he could wait for it to happen out in the street, and get creamed there.

Except there would be no coach, no one to stop Willie if he decided to stomp him as well. Would he really go that far? Benny couldn't predict it. He just knew that it was a risk he didn't want to take.

"How about it?" Benny said. "You can beat the crap out of me in an alley, or you can do it right here in front of everyone."

Willie growled, but then the idea began to appeal to him. "Deal, weasel," he said, and stuck out a huge hand. "You're gonna get yours. You've been asking for it for a long time."

"All right, boys," Cooley said. "Get gloved up. We'll meet back here in fifteen minutes."

The entire gym was crowded. Word seemed to have gone out along the street like wildfire. Everyone and his brother and cousins seemed eager to watch Benny get his head handed to him.

The gloves laced up on his hands made him feel like an idiot. He looked down at his birdlike frame, and then over at Willie's glistening expanse of brown muscles, and realized that this wasn't just a mismatch—this was a mugging.

The bell rang, and Benny left his corner. "Keep your hands up!" Cass said behind him. He did, and just in time, because Willie threw a thunderous right which hit Benny's gloves instead of his face, which Benny found highly preferable.

Jab cross.

Where had *that* thought come from? Benny didn't know, but he was moving out of the way before Willie began to throw it, and—

Hook to body.

Time froze. He could see himself, see the blows, watch his own fist extend, and knew that Willie would run into it, supplying the force needed to provide impact.

He watched as his body did it, as he moved, and moved, and his hand rose almost by itself, and he remembered to plant it squarely in the solar plexus—

Willie went *whoof!* And the air left his mouth in a *whoosh*. An expression like indignation spread over his face, and—

Hook to head.

He saw it, he knew that the opening would be there, but he couldn't *quite* get his body to respond fast enough, and the opening disappeared almost as quickly as it had appeared.

And he knew what was happening. *It* was back, he was seeing things before they happened. He knew what Willie was going to do before Willie *himself* knew. There was only one problem: knowing what to do and being able to do something about it were two entirely different things.

He was able to use his unexpected gift to avoid Willie for most of the first round, that odd precognition pulling him this way and that . . . twice more he saw openings before they appeared, and managed to get his fists up into them. Only one of those times was he able to respond to the timing and leverage necessary to create power—and Willie's feet shot out from under him, and he hit the mat, hard.

The bell rang, and Willie got back up, not hurt, but

embarrassed. The crowd, which had come to watch the local Goliath slay David, was being treated to a spectacle of a different kind.

Benny wobbled back to his corner, huffing. Cass was almost bouncing with glee. "How are you doing that? I didn't know you could box."

"Neither did I," he said.

He looked out at the audience, and met Jenny's eyes. They were embarrassed, and frightened . . . and proud.

Of him.

He put his mouthpiece back in, and bounced back into the center of the ring, feeling as if he was ready to take on the champion of the world.

Rush.

He felt it before it happened, knew that in frustration Willie was going to try to rush him, and moved just to where he needed to be as the bigger boy plowed across the ring, bounced off the ropes, turned and—

Right cross.

With perfect timing, Benny punched, putting everything he had into it, and it landed right squarely on Willie's nose. The *crunch* was clearly audible. Willie staggered back, with an expression on his face something like *how did I get into this?*

Benny whaled on him, throwing rights and rights and lefts, and Willie covered up, dizzy, a flash of genuine confusion and doubt on his face, and the crowd now cheering Benny! Benny! Benny!

Suddenly, and sickeningly, Benny realized that he was getting tired, and that he wasn't hurting Willie at all.

Oops.

Willie pushed him back.

There are immutable realities in the universe: gravity, friction, toast landing butter-side down. In that moment Benny recalled another one. He had first learned it listening to a radio interview with Joe Louis, during which the Brown Bomber had said: "If a boxer had to fight a heavy bag for ten rounds, the heavy bag would win."

Well, Benny hadn't even gone two rounds, six full minutes, before the reality of that came home to him. To put it more bluntly, Benny ran out of gas.

He saw what Willie was going to do,

Cross.

knew *exactly* where it would land—

Head.

He saw the second punch, and the third one, and knew that he would dodge the first two, and then, from sheer fatigue, run right into the third.

Hook.

It wasn't fair.

Be that as it may, it happened anyway. He dodged. And dodged, and then—

"—the winner!" Benny opened his eyes and saw Willie Hawkins's arm being raised in the middle of the ring. He staggered up and extended his hand to Willie.

Hawkins looked at him curiously, something unfamiliar in the bigger boy's face. Then he turned and left the ring without touching gloves, and Benny was alone.

God, he was tired.

"Listen, Benny—you want to get a soda? I'll buy," Cass said as he laced up his shoes.

His jaw hurt like blazes. "Not right now," he muttered. "Maybe later."

She protested, but he kissed her on the cheek—the first time he had ever done that—and said, "Maybe later."

He walked out of the gym, noticing vaguely that some of the kids were staring at him. He managed to wring a smile out of his sore and exhausted muscles when they began a halfhearted round of applause.

He had walked two blocks toward home when he heard someone behind him, calling his name. He turned in time to see Jenny running behind him, her face flushed with the effort. She stared at him, and he saw something in her eyes that he had never dared hoped to see there. Now that he did, he didn't know quite what to think.

"I hate Willie for what he did to you," she said.

She reached out and touched the side of his face. "Does it hurt?" she asked.

"Only when I breathe," he said.

Her eyes were huge. "I think that I live a little closer than you do," she said. "Why don't you let me take care of that for you?"

He took her hand in his. And realized in that moment that they were both outsiders, in their way, and that they were both alone. All of the time that he had known her, had seen her from afar, he had only seen that all the boys wanted to be with her, and had never asked what it would feel like to be *Jenny,* and to know what the boys wanted, and why.

He looked in her eyes, and saw the fire.

"I don't know," he said.

She seemed to have read his thoughts, and she chewed at the fleshiness of her lower lip. "I know," she said. "I know about my reputation, and maybe I deserve it. And it's not like that. You're not like any of the others. You always treated me so good. Kind of like a queen. I ain't no queen, Benny." Her eyes were huge, and chocolate, and bottomless.

"But right now, if you want me, I'll try to be."

He was speechless.

Jenny's apartment building made his look like the Taj Mahal. It was overcrowded, the halls were too narrow, and it stank, as if the residents hadn't bothered to flush for a week. He smelled rank, oily smoke, as from searing fat, and through an open door saw a painfully thin woman frying meat in an iron skillet over a smoking stove. Rags were hung around the kitchen, too damned close to the fire, and he cringed at the sight.

"Pretty, isn't it?" Jenny said, aware of his thoughts. "I'm getting out of here one day. This might be enough for my Momma, but if I can get my grades up, I think I can talk my uncle into taking me in."

She touched her finger to her lips and stopped beside a door on the fifth floor, fished in her pocket for a key then slipped inside, leaving him in the hall. A naked light bulb flickered from a chain overhead, and from somewhere deep in the bowels of the building came the moist syncopation of dripping water.

Jenny emerged a minute later, with a blanket over her arm. She smiled at him shyly, and led him up to the tar-paper covered rooftop. The evening shadows were just stealing over the chimneys. She laid the blanket down for both of them, took his hand and sat him down, kneeling beside him. His throat felt as if it had swollen shut, and he didn't know what to say or do.

She took his hand, and kissed the palm gently.

He finally managed to stammer out: "I've never . . . I mean, this is my first."

"There's a first time for all of us," she said, and leaned forward to kiss him.

For all of his life, he had heard boys and men talking about the secrets between men and women, and had always wondered about them, wondered what the truth might have been. It was different than he had thought it would be. It wasn't the fireworks, it wasn't the sound of trumpets or the clap of thunder. It was something very quiet, and strong, like a current pulling him toward a waterfall, a gentle welcome back to a world long lost, a homecoming.

It wasn't what the boys had said.

It was better.

There was something different about the days that followed. Benny walked taller, strode the streets as if he was a man for the first time. He had survived a fight with the toughest dude in the neighborhood, and even if he lost, he had also bloodied his tormentor's nose. Numbers runners for Big Sid glanced at him as if he was a little crazy, but that didn't bother him—he knew that he was right, he knew that within the next few days it would be proven.

And in the evenings, there was Jenny, and the rooftop, and all of the sweetness that he had ever imagined, and had never truly hoped to find.

Three days after their first time together, Jenny lay close to him, propped up on her elbows on their blanket. Although the sun had set, the air was still warm. They looked out across the city, and its lights, and sounds, and she sighed.

"I want something more, you know?" she said.

He knew. And told her so, with a kiss.

"I want to find something that would make most people think they were dreaming. I have these dreams sometimes. About people and places, you know? There's more to the world than just these few blocks. Can you understand that, Benny?"

Yes.

More than he could say, he understood.

She turned to look at him. "I know what you think, Benny," she said. "You think that you're in love with me. But you're not. And I don't want you to say anything here that you'll feel like you're bound by."

"Jenny—"

"Hush," she said. "This is just for now. Just because you've always been sweet. And if I was to tell you the truth—it wasn't for you. It was for me. There is something special about you. And maybe I've always seen it, always known it, but it's like this summer you learned it yourself. You're just passing though, Benny. You're going to do something special. I just wanted to know that you'd remember me," she said.

The weary fatalism in her voice couldn't completely mask the fierce animal energies slumbering within her. She rolled atop him. "Remember me, Benny," she said. "Promise?"

He nodded. "I promise."

"I want another promise from you."

At that moment, he could not have denied her anything.

"I'm going to say something, and you have to promise not to answer."

He nodded again, silently this time.

"I love you, Benny," she said, and kissed him.

SHUFFLE

CHAPTER
27

1953

TIME PASSED. Sleep and waking melding together into a single flowing reality.

Benny slept, but in sleeping was graced—or cursed—with the same visions that haunted his waking. He woke, lurched directly to the typewriter, opened a hole in his reality and fell into it, into a world of far places and alien ideas, a world far preferable to his own.

Sleeping became waking. Waking was sleeping. The two melded until they were almost indistinguishable. He wasn't certain whether he was a man typing stories of the future on a battered typewriter in a walk-up apartment in 1953 Harlem, or if he was a man who commanded a space station in the twenty-third century, who, in the midst of terrible stress, had begun to dream of a simpler, darker time.

But those two streams of consciousness wove together on a deeper level than they ever had before, and in the depths of the very core of his mind, they met in a place where Benny didn't seem to exist at all.

He dreamed while awake; his fingers became a living creature all their own. They were having their own way with him. He floated back away, up above the dark and driven man hunched above a keyboard.

I'm afraid, he thought.

And he was. This was a place without time, without any connection to meaning as he had understood it all his life. And then he understood that it wasn't new fear that he felt, it was the fear he had always known, now revealing itself to him at a new and deeper level.

What was it that Franklin Roosevelt had once said to his beleaguered people? "There is nothing to fear, but fear itself."

If that was true, then the greatest gift that he could give himself was to own that fear, so that it could teach him.

But his fear took no dark shape. Instead, it was again like the gentle, glowing shape of an hourglass, a gemstone glowing and flowing for his benefit alone.

And this time it spoke to him.

Every man fears, it said. *But not every man looks into his fear. Just as few men truly gaze into the face of the thing that they love. They seek to spare themselves terror or desire by so doing.*

Look onto the streets of your city, and you will see people who have lost touch with that which they love and fear. This is the source of all despair.

I don't understand, Benny said.

The thing you fear you either fight or run from. The thing you love you pursue. Together, they create motion. Together, they combine to drive you toward your future. Look at the children of Africa around you.

There is so much fear in their lives that it seems to surround them, seems to create walls and floor and ceiling, seems to create a tiny box in which they are forced to live out their existence. So they give up trying, and seek to find what happiness they can find within the limitations.

Look at the children of Europe, those who once enslaved your ancestors. Instead of facing the reality and the shame of what once happened, they live in denial. Yet they know how they would long for vengeance if such had been done to them, and they fear what the Africans would do to them if ever they had the chance to strike back. So a portion of their energy is used to hold you back, rather than seek the things they love. Rather than deal with their deeper fears. They cheat themselves, and you.

You cheat yourself, and them.

Who am I, Benny asked, *that you would say such things to me?*

You are the one who will help them remember. Who will help them remember what they fear.

And help them to seek what they love.

SHUFFLE

198

CHAPTER
28

PABST WAS SEATED at his desk, holding one of Benny's stories, extracted from a pile of files stacked before him. The sun streaming through his window bleached the little remaining color from his face. He looked stricken.

"Have you lost your mind?" he asked.

Benny sat in a chair across from him. He seemed consumed by his own inner flame, burnt out. Completely spent. Somehow, he managed to find the strength or self-possession to smile.

"Lately," Benny said, "I've been asking myself the same question."

Pabst looked as if he wanted to cry. "I give you a novella to write—even offered you a shot at the cover. And three weeks later, instead of a novella, you come back with six stories—six sequels to a story I refused to publish in the first place. So I guess the answer to the question we've both been asking is yes—you're certifiable!"

And that moment, Benny couldn't find it within him to say that Pabst was wrong.

In the outer office, Albert, Kay, Julius, and Herbert watched Benny and Pabst from the "Bull Pen." The glass partition prevented them from hearing a word, but the body language was clear. Darlene, who was typing furiously at her desk, muttered without looking up from her machine.

"The old man's not a happy camper," she said.

"Can't blame him, can we?" Julius said.

"Watch me," Herbert said, furious.

Albert searched his pockets for a nonexistent match. "Well, to be fair . . . I mean, after all . . . well, Mister Pabst did tell Benny . . . you know, not to bother him with any more of those . . ."

Herbert looked disgusted. "Whose side are you on?"

"Do we, uh . . . ," he searched an inside pocket, found nothing, and kept looking. "Really have to, you know, pick sides?"

"If we did," Kay sneered, "we all know whose side you'd be on. The robots'."

The door to Pabst's office opened. A dejected Benny emerged.

Herbert was the first to speak. "Let me guess," he said to Benny. "Attila the Nazi said 'no.'"

Benny tried to smile, but failed miserably. "Good guess," he said.

Julius sighed, and drummed his fingers, then a

sudden, half-optimistic light appeared in his eyes. "You might consider putting those stories out yourself—you know, through a private publishing house. A nice, elegant little volume. Fifty to a hundred copies."

For a moment Benny's eyes widened. "I couldn't really do that . . ."

"Why not? Some of our finest men of letters self-published."

Kay was openly derisive. "He may as well write them in chalk on the sidewalk. More people would read them that way."

Herbert struck his palms together, grinning. "Huzzah. You tell him, Kay. I know a good divorce lawyer if you need one."

Albert was lost in thought for a long time. In fact, the entire office seemed to sink into a slumber. The distant sound of car horns outside the window was the only break from the depths of shared despair. Then Albert pursed his lips, muttered to himself, then looked up and said: "I've got an idea. Why not make it . . . you know, a dream?"

The comment was met with stunned silence. It seemed that everyone in the room had literally stopped breathing. For Benny, he wondered if the bottom had fallen out of the world. They all looked at Albert as if they had never seen anything quite like him before.

"Uh . . ." Benny said, not quite certain that he had heard what he thought he had heard. "What's that?"

Albert nodded, his eyes growing almost painfully wide. They all recognized the expression: he was starting to get excited. "Uh, you know . . . make the ending of your first story—'Deep Space Nine'—a dream."

Julius opened his mouth as if about to bray laughter, but then closed it again. "But who's doing the dreaming?" he finally asked, confused.

Kay was watching them, and her anger had dissipated. The lovely dark eyes were sparkling now: Albert's excitement appeared to be infectious. "Someone without much hope," she said. "A shoeshine boy or a convict."

It, whatever the hell it was, the rest of them were catching it like wildfire. Darlene was the next one to chime in. "Whoever it is, they're dreaming of a better tomorrow."

Herbert shook his head, as if already seeing a thousand things wrong with the idea. "Making it a dream guts the whole story."

"I think it makes it more poignant," Julius said.

Herbert wasn't buying—yet. But his sales resistance was definitely weakening. "But what about your other Sisko stories. You can't make them all a dream."

Kay shook her head. She had a clear vision now, and just wouldn't be denied. "Let him get the first one published," she said. "He can worry about the others later."

Hands crossed behind his back, Herbert stalked back and forth across the office, and finally leaned against the wall, watching them. He chewed his lower lip nervously.

"What do you think, Benny?" Julius asked.

"What do I think? I think it's a genius idea . . ."

and yet the growing excitement was tempered by another voice screaming *no, no,* that he was selling his idea out, that he was a traitor to his muse. But finally practicality won out. "I think that it's better than chalk on the sidewalk," he said.

"A hell of a lot better, and once you've gotten the first one past, and there isn't a riot or anything like that, it will be much easier to sell the next one, I can almost guarantee it."

Benny could feel his courage flooding back into him, and the feeling of excitement growing. This could work. It really could!

Before he could talk himself out of it, Benny turned and stalked into Pabst's office. He opened the door, and stood there as Pabst continued to study stacks of paper. The office was always cluttered: Fan mail, bills, sales figures, all of them passed Pabst's desk, and for just a moment Benny's empathy for the man increased. Pabst wasn't the enemy—he was just another working stiff trying to get through the day. And just maybe, they could get through the day together.

Benny cleared his throat, and Pabst looked up, annoyed. "Now what?" he asked.

"I've got a plan," Benny said, and commenced the sales spiel of his life.

Jimmy would have been proud.

CHAPTER
29

THE STREET OUTSIDE was a bustling confusion, the people filling it heading in a hundred different directions and a thousand separate destinies. Sometimes Benny felt lost by the crush, sometimes he just wanted to collar each of them as they walked by and scream: *I'm here! I'm somebody! See me!*

But today, as he left the Trill building, he didn't need them to notice him. They were going to do something far, far better.

They were going to buy his stories.

He was flying, dancing. Someone had sewn wings to his feet, and he was floating on air. Today, he felt like he was the one who the Yankees should put up to bat, not Willie. The way he felt, he would knock that little white ball clean out of the park.

He walked, strode, strutted, almost ran to the train station. It was all that he could do to keep from breaking into song. This was his town, *his* city, and on a day like today, he could do anything in the world.

It was a *great* day.

By the time that Benny got back to Harlem, he could no longer restrain himself. Other passengers on the train must have thought him mad, the way he kept bursting into laughter, talking to himself, eyes locked on some point beyond their focus. This was victory, sweet and simple, and he was intoxicated with it.

He ran down the street, and almost collided with Jimmy, who reacted as if Benny had just caught him stealing a purse. Benny didn't really notice the guilty reaction, and grabbed Jimmy's thin shoulders, shaking with glee. "Hey Jimmy!" he said. "I've got great news. We're headed for the stars!"

Jimmy squinted at him for a minute, but seemed in too much of a hurry to ask what the devil he was jabbering on about. "Yeah, yeah," he said, trying to wriggle out of Benny's grip. "Whatever you say."

Benny was vibrating with joy. "Come on," he bubbled. "I'll buy you a lunch—tell you all about it."

For a moment, Jimmy seemed about to consider it, but then shrugged. "Naw, man," he said. "Later, maybe. I got to take care of some business. I'll see you around."

Jimmy took off. Walking at first, but with a stiff-backed self-consciousness. He stopped, turned around, and glanced back over his shoulder. When he realized that Benny was still watching him, he took off running, faster and faster, his skinny young legs pumping in a blur.

There was so much about Jimmy that reminded Benny of himself. So much that called to him. It wasn't surprising that he wanted to help the boy. . . . but that thought was followed almost instantly by another: something about Jimmy's behavior set the alarm bells jangling.

He considered following his young friend, but abandoned the notion. With every moment, the alarm grew more and more distant, until it was a puny thing, much smaller than the happiness swelling within him. He would talk to Jimmy another time. Later. Now, he wanted to share his good news, and he needed to do it with just the right person, right now.

Willie Hawkins leaned across the counter, his thick forearms crossed, muscles bunched and bulging as he spoke in his rapid-fire way, trumpeting his achievements to Cassie as if he could never, ever get enough of his own voice. And perhaps he couldn't, at that.

"—bottom of the seventh," he was saying, "I came up again. And on an oh-two fast ball—*BAM!*" He mimed the strike, his hawk eyes narrowed as if following a tortured baseball far up into the heavens. "Into the bleachers. Had to be at least four hundred feet."

Cassie kept wiping the counter, but paused to acknowledge the majesty of Willie's achievement with a nod of her head. "I know all about it, Willie," she said. "I read the newspaper."

"Yeah," Willie said. "But you gotta admit—they don't tell it as well as I do."

She had to laugh at that, and her giggles reached their peak as Benny entered. Benny just stood in the doorway, staring at them, and waiting there with an expression on his face that Cassie found almost impossible to define. Something infinitely self-satisfied, bubbling with pride, something . . .

Willie was oblivious to it. He turned. "Hey, man," Willie said. "Hear the game last night? I went two for four."

Benny nodded happily. "That's great, Willie," he said sincerely. "But I went *four* for four."

He placed his hands on the counter, vaulting it as lightly as a sixteen-year-old track star. He landed with barely a sound. Cassie stared at him as if he had gone crazy. He hugged her soundly, whooping.

"They're publishing one of my Sisko stories!"

She was stunned, beginning to smile, but stayed silent. By the way that he had said it she could tell that there was more good news to come.

And there was. "And at three cents a word!"

She hugged him back enthusiastically. "Good for you, baby."

"Tonight," he announced, "we're celebrating. Dinner, dancing—the works."

He looked at her and saw the woman that he loved, and the girl he had known most of his life. How long had she waited to see him so happy? To hear him say the words that would change her life? Perhaps tonight would be the night. Yes. That felt right. Tonight would be the night everything changed.

"I'll wear my red dress," she said finally.

"You're damned right you will."

When he kissed her, there was no thought of a gawking Willie, or the staring customers. No thought but her softness and sweetness.

And the stars within him, waiting to be born.

That night he didn't forget, nor did he oversleep, nor work, nor was he called away for an emergency. A sudden mood swing didn't prevent their outing, and Harlem didn't erupt into sudden riots to stop them from having the promised evening on the town.

Instead, there was dinner at Maxie's, with steak and homemade bread, and afterwards there were drinks at the New Crest, and dancing so sweet and intoxicating that Benny thought that he would lose his mind.

In every glance, every touch, Cassie was speaking to him without words. *You're the man I love,* she was saying. *I've loved you longer than you know. Just stay with me a little while longer and we'll find each other. It can happen for us, and the old ghosts can rest where they belong.*

They emerged after what seemed like the longest, most delicious night of his life into a night in which the sky had been swept clean by a light rainfall. The stars in it shone down brightly, their approval a full and joyous thing. And all was right in the world.

Cassie was beautiful in her dress. It clung to her curves as though it had been spun upon her body by a magic loom. Benny's hand rested proprietarily upon her waist. It felt warm and comfortable there. As if it belonged there. As if they belonged together. Finally, he realized, he was beginning to lower some of the barriers that had made him keep her at a distance.

You don't marry a woman like Cassie unless you can offer her stability. She's a worker, and if she committed to you, and your career failed, she would work to keep you afloat, work until her beauty was gone, until the passion was gone, until all that remained was her commitment to a promise she should never have made. You couldn't do that to her. But now, now that everything is happening . . .

Maybe this is the time.

Benny took her into his arms, and whirled her once around the sidewalk. She giggled, and let him spin her, moving to the music drifting from the door of a nearby club. A couple passing on the other side of the street watched them dubiously, but for the moment, he could ignore them, ignore everything, except the sensation of being completely, utterly alive.

For a few moments he was able to forget everything, forget the pain and the long years, and all of the dreams he had always feared might never come true.

The flow of the fantasy was marred only by a sudden flare of pain in her face, and she broke away from him and hobbled over to a streetlight. Even through the evident pain, she still laughed.

"My poor feet," she said, massaging them. "Baby, you better marry me soon. I'm not getting any younger."

He turned, spinning, and took her in his arms. Then he stopped and gazed deeply into her eyes. "But you are getting more and more beautiful," he said, and she sighed, leaning her head against his chest.

She tilted her lips up to meet his, and he felt the hours and days and years lifting away, floating away and away as if none of them mattered at all, and beneath them was a contentment like nothing that he had ever known.

"Cassie," he murmured. "I love—"

"Brother Benny—" a voice said behind them, and she opened her eyes and looked around to see the tall and imposing figure of the man that they called only the Preacher.

He walked toward them on legs that seemed somewhat rickety, but with something burning in his eyes that was like a fire from heaven. He looked like a black Gabriel, come to ring the sinful time of man to a close. Cassie shied away from him, but Benny smiled and greeted him. "Preacher," he said. "I was hoping I'd see you again."

"Were you, Brother Benny?"

"Yes," he paused, ever the natural storyteller. "I did it," he said. "My story's going to be published."

The Preacher threw his head back and his arms wide and intoned, "'The light of the Lord is in his path.'" There was something that a normal person might have called a smile on the Preacher's face, but when he looked back at them, it had vanished. "Brother Benny," he said, and his voice dropped down to a low growl. "This is only the beginning of your journey—not the ending. And the path of the Prophets sometimes leads into darkness and pain."

Benny stiffened at this, as though the Prophets had struck him physically. A quick stab of fear stole some of the pleasure from the night.

"Benny," Cassie said. "What's he talking about?" When Benny couldn't, or wouldn't answer, she turned to the Preacher. "Who are you, really? How can you say things like this, spoil our evening?"

Her gaze might have withered an oak, but the Preacher was unfazed. "I speak with the voice of the Prophets," he said.

The Preacher reached out and grabbed Benny's ear before Benny could flinch away. There was a sharp stab of pain. "Hey!" he said, but before he could react further, the Preacher took his hand away and stared at it.

By the light of the streetlight, Benny could see the blood smeared on the Preacher's hand.

Benny touched his ear fearfully, but when he brought his hand back before his face, there was no blood on it at all. It must have been an illusion. A trick.

"And in their words," the Preacher said, "hope and despair walk arm in arm." He held Benny's gaze with his own, as if he had emerged from his madness just long enough to relay a message from some other world. Without another word, leaving them on that ominous note, the Preacher walked away. Benny and Cassie watched him go wordlessly.

"Did you understand any of that?" Cassie said.

Before Benny could answer, something split the night air, a sound as sharp and hard as the sound of a

New Year's firecracker. Benny jerked as if struck. After a pause, there were three more shots, one after another.

She paused, and glanced at him. "Is that gunfire?"

"Sounds like it," he said slowly.

A few people ran past them, in the direction of the gunshots. The Preacher had reached the end of the block, closer to the sounds of violence. His face, caught in the oblique light of the street lamp, seemed wreathed in fire. "The time has come, Brother Benny," he called out. "Go and 'be of good courage.'"

Cassie tried to tug him in the opposite direction, but Benny was already moving.

"Baby," she said. "No. Not that way. Let's go home. Please."

"I can't," Benny said. He was like a sleepwalker now, like a man caught in a dream he cannot control. "I have to find out." He followed the stream of people who were heading toward the sounds. They were normal people, people who might have entered Eva's Kitchen seeking a burger or a cup of java. Now, they were hungry for something else. Now, they needed to see what the violence was, as if witnessing it directed toward another might postpone the inevitable, ultimate violence of their own fates.

Benny looked stricken. He didn't want to do this, didn't want to see what lay at the end of the street, but couldn't help himself, was pulled along as if by a tide. And he pulled Cassie along with him, the warmth and comfort of the meal so recently shared forgotten and all replaced by the fear that he was about to see something that would change the night. Change everything. Change his own essence. Forever.

Two police cars were parked at right angles to the sidewalk. There was a swarm of uniformed officers keeping the crowd at bay, and Benny felt the breath in his throat bubbling and burning as if he was trying to breathe through a throat full of molten lava.

In the middle of the street, he saw two officers that he knew. He had seen these men before. They had stopped him outside the *Incredible Tales* offices. They had stepped on his picture. They had done what they could to steal his dignity from him. And now they guarded the still and silent body of a boy. They angled themselves as if trying to keep him from getting a good view, and his heart roared in his chest.

"Stay back—" one of the officers said.

But Benny circled, stooping, hypnotized, seeking to get a closer look, already knowing what he would find, what he would have to find.

He recognized the face, still now in death. Recognized the hands that he had held in infancy, the face that had laughed so often. He knew the true color and texture of the fluid leaking from beneath him, black as tar in the streetlight, flowing stickily into the gutter.

He knew that it was insane, but somehow the thought came to him that if he could just avoid seeing what he knew there was to see, just not admit what he had to admit, not speak the name even now coming to his tongue, that somehow the awful reality would not be, could be undone. The moment he spoke the word, by some arcane magical principles the violent actions of these blind and brutal men would suddenly take on a deeper, truer reality, and that would be the end of hope.

"Jimmy," he murmured, his heart breaking.

Benny moved toward the body, but officer Ryan blocked his approach, shoving him away.

"Get the hell back," Ryan said. He tried to block Benny's approach with his own body, using that barrel chest as if it was a mobile shield.

Benny felt a red haze rising up to steal reason from him. "What happened?" Benny asked.

"What's it to you?" Ryan challenged. Benny wasn't certain, but thought he smelled liquor on the man's breath.

Benny tried to keep Jimmy's limp form in sight. He wasn't just looking at a boy's corpse. He was looking at the living boy he had been yesterday, and the day before that, and the day before that. All of the Jimmies that Benny had ever known, reduced to this one inanimate lump here, on the street.

And he watched another string of Jimmies, the Jimmy that *might* have been, stretched out in another endless chorus line. There were a myriad of them. There was a doctor Jimmy, and a carpenter Jimmy. There were simple men who toiled at work gladly, returning at night to the arms of good women who loved them and healed the hurt of hearts that often labored in darkness.

There were bad Jimmies, too, Jimmies that had never learned the meaning of honest work, Jimmies that stole what they could not, or would not earn. Yes, those Jimmies were there as well.

And he knew them all, and loved them all, and watched those future Jimmies winking out, fading out . . .

One.

After another.

After another.

Until all that remained was the limp and lifeless form of the Jimmy which would never be anything again but meat, who would run no races, who would share no laughter, whose lifeblood even now drained meaninglessly into the gutter.

Jimmy. Dead.

"I know him," Benny said numbly.

The other cop came over, carrying with him his nightstick and gun, his arrogant swagger and obscene self-confidence. Cloaked, armed with all of that, and more. "Yeah?" Mulkahey said harshly. "Then maybe you can explain what he was doing trying to break into that car."

Mulkahey pointed to a sedan. A Ford, made in the late forties. Worth maybe a few hundred dollars, maybe as much as a thousand. There were a few items in the back seat of the car, visible even from across the street. A coat. A package wrapped in brown paper. A bag of groceries. Whatever their monetary value, their ultimate worth had been the life of a young man.

Benny's mind whirled. He turned to the two cops, terrified of the darkness within him. "Is that why you shot him? For breaking into a *car?*"

Ryan almost, almost managed to conceal his smile. "He tried to run," he said, as if that explained it.

The pounding in Benny's ears rang so strongly that

he could barely hear anything, any more, so that he was almost unable to hear the murmur of his own thoughts. He was angry, he was frustrated, he was pushed to some place outside his control. He tried to push past them, to see for himself, to see more closely, and the darkness swirled and swirled and—

SHUFFLE

CHAPTER
30

BENJAMIN SISKO stood on the Promenade of the space station known as Deep Space Nine. He looked down, incredulously at the body laying limp and unmoving on the floor.

The burnt-coffee skin, the face he had kissed so many times, the eyes which were the only remnants of the woman he had loved and lost. He felt as if they were plunging down a hole, falling away from him. His son was dead.

Jake Sisko was dead.

He felt a great and terrible fire stirring within him, one which would not bend to logic, nor yield to reason. Over his son's body stood Gul Dukat and Weyoun. Their faces held no remorse, betrayed no sorrow. If anything, they had not quite managed to conceal their contempt, their glee that they had finally managed to strike so dear a blow.

"You murdered him," Sisko said. "You murdered my son!"

Weyoun sneered. "He refused to obey a direct order," he said.

Dukat took a combat-ready stance. "He got exactly what he deserved," he said, his eyes daring Sisko to act.

Without knowing how or when he had begun the action, Sisko was in the air, burying his fingers in Dukat's throat. Despite the Cardassian's readiness, despite his long combat experience, Sisko's speed and ferocity caught him by surprise, and he went down hard. Sisko was atop him in a moment, all of the rage and frustration and hatred that only a mourning parent can feel boiling out of him in one savage moment.

But before Sisko could truly press his advantage, Weyoun had stepped around him, hitting him over the head with the butt of a phaser. Sisko's knees buckled, and he spilled to the side.

Dukat rolled to his knees, then stood unsteadily. Sisko flew at him again, all of his combat training forgotten, remembering only that the son he had nurtured and loved was gone. Gone. Only the feel of Gul Dukat's bones breaking beneath his hands could possibly give him satisfaction, now or ever again.

Weyoun hit him again, and then again. Sisko groaned, falling down, and then Dukat and Weyoun were on him, driving him into the ground, pummeling him, stomping, screaming, cursing, and the blows went on and on and on like bloody raindrops in an endless black typhoon.

Benjamin Sisko flinched away from another terrible

blow, but saw a woman who looked much like Kasidy Yates, but wasn't. She wore clothes that were . . . strange.

And her name was . . . Cassie. Yes, Cassie.

"Stop it!" She screamed. Yes, she did. "Stop it! You're killing him."

As unconsciousness rose to claim him, Benjamin Sisko finally remembered, that he wasn't a Starfleet officer after all. He wasn't a man of honor and responsibility. He was a small, unimportant man named Benny Russell, a black man in a white man's world, being beaten to death in the middle of the street as a hundred white people watched, and not one lifted a hand to help him.

SHUFFLE

CHAPTER
31

"Stop it!" Cassie pleaded.

No one listened. No one acted. There was no one who gave a damn. She turned, in horror, to see the faces. Faces of people who, in another time, as individuals, might have treated her with respect and kindness. Faces of people who, in this time and space, did not, could not afford to care.

With all of the strength in her slender body, she tried to intervene, but she was pulled away by one of the other officers, who held her fast and watched as the beating continued.

The tears rose in her throat to become something deeper, something even more painful. And she was sobbing now, pleading, as if she didn't even know who she was any more. Certainly, no sane being would want to be a part of this one. Anywhere but here. Screaming for help that did not come, she watched the only man she had ever loved reduced to an insensate, bleeding pulp against the cold and glistening sidewalk.

SHUFFLE

CHAPTER
32

1940

BIG SID'S CAR came for Benny at five o'clock. It was a limousine that seemed to be a block long. Sid's bodyguard, a gigantic ex-pro boxer who claimed to have been one of Joe Louis' sparring partners, opened the door for him personally.

Ardelia and Benny sat in the back seat as they were taken to the spacious apartment up on Sugar Hill, to be welcomed by an expansive, gold-toothed, smiling Sid.

"Benny!" Sid said. "Benny my boy, you did it!" There was a pile of bills on the table, and Benny's eyes opened wide to see them. His aunt whooped and swooped down on them, stuffing them in her purse eagerly.

"I knew it!" she cried, the expression on her face so predatory that Benny quailed inside. "I told you this boy could do it!"

"All the money is there," Sid said. He watched Benny, his tight little eyes cautious within the folds of fat. "Sit down, boy. Sit down, and let's talk. I seen you grow up, boy—always thought there might be something unusual about you. And now I think maybe there is."

He pointed to the pile of money in front of him. "I made a hunch—you've got to do that in this business. I decided to trust you, see if you paid off. I laid *fifty* dollars a day on your number, and after five days it paid off." He leaned forward. "I got a feeling that we can do business—"

Benny heard the words, saw the money, felt pride and excitement swelling within him. He had done it! He really did have the power! And he could use it again and again and—

(The stove)

What in the hell was *that* image? And why did he suddenly smell burning fat?

Big Sid was still jabbering, "—when you get another dream, I'm going to take a chance. This here is found money, so if I bet it, and maybe another hundred on the side—"

Again that smell. This time stronger. Hell—Sid's luxurious apartment had, narrowed, darkened, collapsed into a filthy, crowded tenement slum, with a smoking

(stove)

now belching smoke, and rags that were beginning to flame—

(Second floor. He saw it. The stink of burning

223

carpet, flaming drapes was enough to choke him now. And he saw the fire spill out into the hallway—)

"We lay off the bets careful, like, spread them around, but as soon as we're sure—"

(He actually *saw* the flames lick to life, saw the old wallpaper blossom with flame, heard the first screams of panic—)

"—got some people who can make bets uptown—," suddenly they were staring at him. "Boy? Benny? Can you hear me, boy?"

Benny suddenly stood up. "I got to go."

His aunt was on her feet. "Benny. This is an important meeting—"

"I've got to go!" Benny said, and he was on his feet, with both of them calling after him, screaming his name. He was out the front door, down the street, not sure where he was going or what he was doing, only that he had to run and run, and he could smell the

smoke

and feel the

heat

and hear the

screams

He didn't know what to do, or what to think, or anything at all except—

Run

CHAPTER

33

By the time he got to Jenny's building, it was completely engulfed in flames. The fire engines blocked off the entire street, and faces in the crowd gazed up at the inferno with expressions that he had known all his life.

Fear.

Empathy.

Relief.

"Is everybody out?" he asked.

One of the firemen rushed past him, his cheeks grimy with ash. A gust of steam opened from the top of the building.

Water played up there, and as water touched superheated brick, steam gushed anew. Then the smoke was caught by a gust of hot air: for an instant parted like storm clouds before the wind. In that moment of sudden clarity he saw a face, pale against the flames, staring out at them from the fifth floor. A face distended with fear, bright with heat, eyes wide with terrible knowledge.

He didn't, couldn't let himself know who it was, or what it meant.

The face turned, madly, smoke gushing from her open mouth. It searched the crowd, until, for a brief moment, she locked eyes with Benny.

She said something. It might have been "Help me." It might have been "Oh God."

It might have been "remember me, Benny."

And then she jumped.

He didn't remember any of the rest of that night. He wandered. He took a train.

He eventually made his way back out to Flushing Meadow. The entire park was covered with trucks and workmen. Most of the empty buildings were being disassembled, although some few of them might stand for another hundred years.

Unnoticed, he made his way to the abandoned Hall of Nations.

Nothing. Everything had been removed. In the alcove of the exhibit donated by the Mali Republic, where the Orb had been, nothing remained but bare walls and floor.

Whatever strength had sustained Benny drained from him utterly, and he collapsed. He curled up on the floor under it, desperately trying to feel something of what had been there, tried to recapture some small scrap of the *knowing* he had experienced only weeks before.

He cried until his eyes had no more tears.

And then he slept.

This time, he did not dream.

CHAPTER
34

IN THE MORNING, Benny was found by workmen. "Hey kid," they said. "What are you doing here?"

"I don't know," he said honestly. All of the memories were slipping away from him, even the precise events of the previous day. Was Jenny really dead? Had a strange gem from another land really spoken to him? Surely, it was all just a dream . . .

"You better get out of here, before we call the cops."

He looked at them, and nodded.

"Have you got money to get home?" an older man asked. His face was densely freckled, his red hair tinged with gray but his eyes were kind.

Benny shook his head. "I'm not even sure how I got here."

The workmen looked at each other. "Harlem?" one asked.

"127th," he said.

The redhead dug in his pants, and pulled out ten cents. "One of these days, I'll see you on the street," he said. "And you better have my dime."

Benny nodded dumbly, and ran, all the way to the station.

The rest of the summer passed too quickly. Benny rarely left his aunt's apartment. Ardelia pled with him to give her another number, but his dreams were black and empty spaces, dead as the void between the stars and he had nothing to give her.

Little Cass came to see him a couple of times. They sat in the living room together, not touching, rarely talking, just keeping company. She tried to pull him into conversations, speaking of boxing or the fair, of things around the neighborhood. He felt as if he sat at the bottom of a well. When he heard her at all, her words were like the wind whispering across its open mouth. Even when he heard her, he couldn't find the strength to answer.

So they sat together. After a few days, he found the strength to take her hand.

The seasons changed, and classes started again. Wearily, Benny dressed and pulled himself out of the house, then entered the red brick building where he would spend his final semester . . . or maybe just a few useless days. He had a notion that perhaps he should just quit. Just stop now. There seemed to be no purpose to life. Vaguely, he remembered that he had seen things, strange things, during the summer, but for the life of him he couldn't remember what. If he could only remember, even a little bit, it might make the difference. But that empty place in his memory was like an open drain, pulling his heart and soul down in a relentless whirlpool of depression.

His fifth period composition class was an ugly surprise. There, large as life, sitting in the front row, was Willie. The boy didn't look at Benny, but he knew that there was unfinished business between them, and Willie would find a way to finish it.

The teacher, a pale woman who looked desperately in need of sunshine, rose and spoke. "Hello. I'm Mrs. Elaine. I am replacing Mr. Cooley in senior composition this year."

One of the girls in the class raised her hand. "Where is Mr. Cooley?"

She hawed and seemed to turn her nose up a bit. "The school administration felt that he was offering too *advanced* a curriculum . . . that is, a course of study for the students at this school. They feel that something suited to future tradesmen would be more appropriate. Many of you will be carpenters. Plumbers." She smiled. "I don't think we have many future poets here."

There was no comment from them, and she went on. "Well. But we will see. I would like you to write an essay for me, just a hundred words on what you did this summer."

Benny took his pencil, and stared at his paper for a couple of minutes. Nothing came, only void.

Only blackness.

As dark as the space between the stars.

He wanted so desperately to say something, if not for himself, for Jenny, whose eyes had begged him to remember her. And in that moment, the moment his attention was off his own pain, and had fastened on his urge to give to someone else—

don't be greedy

The universe opened up to him. Not the torrent which had come before. Just a trickle . . . a single ray of light in his darkness.

It was enough.

After a half hour, Mrs. Elaine said, "well, halt." She smiled primly, and Benny found himself absently wondering what *Mr.* Elaine looked like. "I was wondering," she said, "if any of you would care to read what you have just written."

There was a general silence in the classroom, then all eyes turned back to Benny. He stood, eyes averted downward. He held a ragged piece of notebook paper in his right hand. Barely moving his lips, he began to read.

"This summer," he said, "Was the worst and best time of my life. This summer I fell in love. This summer, the girl I've loved all my life said that she loved me. This summer I watched her die." He paused, and realized that his eyes were hot, and streaming, that his voice had cracked. "This summer my heart broke, but my mind opened. I saw what I was, and what I might be one day. I know that I don't have to be a carpenter, or a plumber, or a number runner. Maybe I'm a poet. Maybe I'll walk in the stars. I might be any of those things, because I am strong, and brave, and I have endured throughout the ages. I'm not what my aunt wants me to be. I'm not what my teachers say I am. I'm not what my friends think I am. I don't know who or what I am anymore, except I know I have dreams, and I'm going to live them." He paused, then repeated, softer this time. "I'm going to live them."

He sat down. The class was silent, until Mrs. Elaine cleared her throat. "Well. That's very interesting, Benny." She studied him as if she had never seen anything quite like Benny before, and then sighed, unwrinkling her pallid brow.

"Well," she said. "Next?"

CHAPTER
35

BENNY WAS WALKING HOME from school later that day. He felt that something had lifted off his chest, as if he had turned some corner in his life, and even if he couldn't define what it was, that didn't make it any less important.

There was a figure leaning up against the wall ahead, and he drew closer to it before he recognized it as Willie. The larger boy was just staring straight ahead, with an expression more contemplative than Benny had ever seen before. Then Willie turned and looked at him.

"I heard what you read, man," he said, quietly.

Benny tensed, waiting. "Yes."

"I didn't love her," Willie said. "None of us did." He stared out across the street, and Benny wondered what he was looking at. Was he remembering Jenny's laughter? Her eyes? The years he had shared with her?

"I didn't love her, but I liked her." He paused. "And you know? I never even told her that. And I should have."

Willie sighed and pushed himself away from the wall. "Nice essay, man. You got a talent for that stuff." He turned and started to walk away, then turned again. "Oh, and by the way—nice right hook." His broad face split in a surprisingly soft grin. "Good fight, man," Willie said, and he held out his hand.

Benny took it, and they shook. Willie's hand was strong and broad and warm.

Willie broke the shake and stuck his hands deep into his pockets. "Which way you going?" he asked, unnecessarily. They knew. They had walked the same way every day for years.

The two boys walked together for a couple of blocks not talking, just sharing the day, until Willie turned right to go to ball practice. "See you around," he said, and once again, more sadly this time, he smiled. Benny watched him, sensing some great and nameless burden lifting from his own chest.

He felt odd. Free, somehow. The world seemed a brighter, wider place, filled with possibilities. For instance, what should he do with the rest of his afternoon?

Benny knew he could go see Big Sid. There was a number runner job open, and Ardelia had made it clear that Sid was interested in keeping the boy close at hand. No, that didn't feel right.

The movies? There was a double bill: *Gone With the Wind* playing with a *Flash Gordon* chapter play, he thought. The idea didn't appeal to him. But what did?

Flash Gordon. The stars. Something about the stars.

Benny turned around, heading back toward the school, thinking about the library. The library, and all of its reference books.

For some reason that he couldn't quite understand, he wanted to find the location of a star called "Sirius."

SHUFFLE

CHAPTER
36

1953

FOR MOST OF NEW YORK, life continued unabated. Shows opened and closed on Broadway, the Empire State Building continued to light up the sky at night. The Statue of Liberty stood immortal in the harbor, holding her torch high in defense of liberty. Times Square churned with life, a twenty-four hour circus, top-heavy with monkeys and clowns.

Millions of people lived their lives, loved their loves, fought their own demons, each enmeshed in his own world, his own existential dilemmas. People care as much as they can, but ultimately each of us lives, and dies, alone.

A city is a nest, a hive, millions of separate minds blended into a superbeing, larger than any one of them, and uninvolved in the lives of any one—a creature ultimately concerned only with its own existence. Those who contribute to its existence are rewarded, regardless of their morality or worth. And those who act contrary to its survival—or those who it thought, in whatever way a living city might think—act contrary to its survival are punished regardless of the righteousness of their cause.

Every living organism craves homeostasis. Upset its internal equilibrium, and it will strike back. Its weapons are many: hormones, antibodies, enzymes. Ultimately, it doesn't matter if the intruder, the betrayer, the guilty cell is a phagocyte, a virus, a cancer, a germ, or a Negro man named Benny Russell.

The body must defend itself, or it will die. The body lives in fear.

Winter came to New York. Although the wind had grown cold, the first snowflakes had yet to fall. Thanksgiving came, with its happiness and family cheer, and throughout the city, an awareness that another year had been survived was summoning the traditional holiday spirit.

There are those who say (cynically, of course) that the major drive of the holiday seasons is our own memories of a time simpler by far, when we, as children, remembered being cared for, and loved. A time when there were far fewer responsibilities. A time when our parents produced food, shelter, and clothing as if by magic. In that simpler world the concept of an elf easing down our chimneys to bring gifts to the good children, and lumps of coal to the bad was somehow palatable. The fact that that idea is inextricably tied up with the subliminal notion that those who *have* are good and those who *do not have* are bad was something that rarely detracted from the enjoyment of the holidays—the idea that Santa seemed to give more to the children of the wealthy than to the poor, more to American children than to those of other nations, more to whites than to blacks . . . this all seemed part of a proper universal order, never really to be questioned, as if the act of questioning itself brought misery into the world.

The decorations began on Broadway, with the extravagance of Macy's Thanksgiving Day parade, with giant floats and stupendous toys of every description nodding and waving to a smiling crowd, floating above and crawling below, giant, swollen slogans of consumer delight.

And little black children watched the parade, wondering: *where am I?*

Where am I?

And no one thought to answer that question.

No one seemed to care. Nor would they, for another entire generation. That day would come, but for now, it seemed so achingly distant, so blindingly remote that, from the vantage of the year 1953, it seemed far beyond the stars themselves.

The joys of the holiday season reached also as far as Harlem, where the irony of worshipping a white Jesus was entirely lost on the churchgoers who stood in myriad storefronts, or in the great Episcopal edifice of Saint Phillips, or the Baptist fortress of Redeemer's Blood Church of Faith. There they sang spirituals, or gospel, or hymns every bit as solemn and traditional as those sung in white communities across America. They worshipped the same God, prayed to the same angels, and dreamt of the same heaven. And if they wondered why that God might have sent His only son to the land of their oppressors, they rarely questioned it. All questions would be answered in the next life. In this realm, this vale of tears, there were challenges to faith, but that is all that they were. The faithful had to learn to absorb these challenges, and still find their way in a strange and sinful world.

The alternative was unthinkable.

And so it was that Christmas music drifted up from the street as far as Benny's apartment that day, almost a month after his savage beating.

For that time, he had tossed in nightmare and fever, he had at times screamed out to the four walls around him that something was coming, coming, but nothing came.

He screamed that it wasn't fair, that Jimmy shouldn't have been taken from the world, shouldn't have been killed without a trial, and of course he shouldn't have been, but that was merely the way things were.

The world wasn't fair. The world wasn't unfair. The world merely was, and human beings, young and old, male and female, Negro and white, merely made their way in it as best they could, and much of the strife therein came from failing to see that we were, after all, merely human, and not the angels we aspire to be.

We are people, sometimes lost in loneliness and

fear, and sometimes striking out from the depths of those feelings, sometimes destroying what we fear, but often killing what we love . . .

Or could have loved, had we but known to open our eyes.

Moving like an old man, Benny dressed himself. Cassie watched him, not moving, not doing him the disservice of coddling him. He wouldn't want that, didn't need that. He had begun walking again only a week before, as if he had newly grown legs or recently thrown away crutches.

It was only when swollen fingers failed to meet the challenge of knotting the tie that she came to him wordlessly, and gave him the aid that he couldn't request. She whipped through a half-Windsor knot, and adjusted the tie as if she had been doing this all of her life, and then helped him on with his jacket.

He looked lumpy, somehow, as if the beating had changed his shape, rearranged the bones beneath his skin. He examined his image in a mirror, and groaned.

"I don't know. I'm not ready for this yet."

She shook her head, and kissed him lightly on the cheek. "I'm telling you baby," she said. "You've been cooped up in this apartment too long. Going down to the office will do you a world of good."

He sighed deeply and almost painfully. "I suppose I should be there when the first copies of the January issue are delivered."

"Absolutely," she said, and pushed as much of her high spirits to the fore as she could. "Didn't you say that the Christmas issue was special? That this was going to be the beginning of big things for you?"

He needed to hear her—or someone—say that, or things like it. He was far, far too close to the edge of his life. And the only tool she had to bring him back was love. "After all the work you did, you deserve to see your story in print," she smiled. "Just don't get too excited. I wouldn't want you to hurt yourself."

Benny smiled as if he had to pull the corners of his lips up with wires. Then the artifice melted. "I'll restrict myself to a proud grin," he said.

They kissed for a beat. Then Cassie pulled back from him, studying. "You're not having any more of those . . . hallucinations, are you?"

He shook his head. This had been a problem. She had told him that during fevers, he had occasionally called out strange names, sometimes called her "Kasidy" instead of "Cassie." That he didn't seem to recognize where they were, acting as if his apartment was something called the "infirmary."

"I'm fine," he lied.

Cassie nodded her head slowly, and then let him go. Ultimately, he had to heal, or die, on his own. There was only so much that any woman's heart could do. For a woman like Cassie, that had to be the hardest lesson in the world.

They were interrupted by a tiny squeaking sound, and then the rustle of little rodent feet scampering across the floor. Benny groaned, and turned in time to see a fat gray shape disappearing into a closet.

She shuddered. "Baby, I really wish you'd get on your landlord. He needs to call the exterminator."

Benny was nodding agreement, when her last word suddenly popped back into his head. *The Exterminator.* Or some title very much like it. Images were suddenly flooding into his mind. "Hey," he said. "I just got an idea for another story. There's this killer robot, and maybe some time travel."

"And I suppose there's a Negro starship captain?" Cassie joked.

"No . . . but maybe there's a Negro scientist. Well meaning, but something goes wrong, and he almost destroys the world. An implacable, killer robot . . ." He mused.

"Didn't you tell me your friend Albert said robots couldn't hurt people? One of his laws or something?"

"You're right," he said, brow beetling. "All right then, it's half-robot and half human. Humans have no trouble killing each other at all."

Some of the old Benny seemed to have returned, and her heart rejoiced. She kissed him lightly. "Break a leg," she said.

"I'll be back," he replied.

The trip downtown to the Arthur Trill Building frightened Benny. He watched the people on the train, the faces growing increasingly pale as he traveled south. He knew that they wondered about him, wondered who he was and what he was doing traveling in their city, wondering what he wanted, and whether he represented a threat to them. He wondered what they would think if they knew that he was more frightened of them than they could possibly be of him.

He got off the train at the right station, and limped

through the crowd, striving to ignore the pain in his hip, and the constant ringing sound in his ear. He hoped that it would eventually go away, but couldn't be sure. He couldn't be sure of anything any more.

But there was one thing that he knew, and that was that the Sisko stories were the best he had ever done, and that if people would just read them, they would make a difference. If people would just give them a chance.

He walked down the street with his mind divided, a part of him thinking about the world of his dreams, and another part keeping an eye open for the men who had nearly crippled him. What would he do if he ran into them on the street? More importantly, what would *they* do?

There had been no inquiry, no official or unofficial sanctions. As far as almost everyone was concerned, Benny was an uppity Negro who had interfered with police business, and gotten what he deserved. The cops had lied, and said that he fought back, that he had brandished weapons, and the other cops had winked and nodded.

If only it could have been recorded, he thought. If only someone had cared enough to make a film, certainly they would never have gotten away with something like that. Maybe in the future, every street-light would have cameras built in, and the police would have to be more careful . . .

And his mind began to spin off another story, and he was happy for that, having begun to wonder if he would ever regain the facility for writing. It was unutterably satisfying to find that part of him beginning to function again.

And if it was, if that *what-if* spark that had sustained him through so many years had begun to work again, then why didn't he apply it to his life?

What if he and Cassie got married?

If only his stories were as popular as he knew they were capable of being, he would be able to afford to take care of her, to build a home.

Yes, a home.

And, *if this goes on,* he would eventually be able to let go of everything, every aspect of his past that had haunted him, and truly look forward to the future, not merely write about it.

And wouldn't *that* be wonderful.

By the time he had reached the *Incredible Tales* building, he was actually in a good mood, managing to put many of his doubts and most of his fears behind him.

He forced himself to walk up the stairs, despite the pain, knowing that the exercise would be good for him. Benny was blowing air by the time he reached the right floor.

The office door yielded to a touch, and he was happy to see that the usual gang was there in the bull pen: Albert, Kay, Julius, and Herbert, talking and rousting each other as usual. Darlene sat at her desk, typing. They looked up and around variously as Benny entered.

Herbert was first to greet him. "Hey Benny," he said. "Long time no see!"

They gathered around, congratulating him on his

recovery and expressing their regret with his recent problems. Benny politely accepted their congratulations, but couldn't wait to get to the only question which really absorbed him. "Is it here?" he asked.

Julius shook his head. "Not yet," he said. "Pabst is still at the printers."

"But," Kay said enthusiastically, "we're all waiting for his return with baited breath."

Albert turned to Benny. "We heard . . . you know, that you were . . . ah . . . ," he began vaguely searching his pockets for a match.

"We heard you got the crap beat out of you," Kay said, finishing Albert's line. Albert looked embarrassed, but nodded.

The embarrassment seemed to spread through the office. What do you say to a man who was almost killed by the very people supposedly responsible for his welfare? Benny let them off the hook, shrugging.

"I'm okay," he said, and handed Albert a lighter.

Albert took it gladly, and began to puff. "Glad to see that you're . . . ah . . . you know, up . . . and about," he said vaguely between draws.

Darlene looked up from her typing, her face excited. "Tell him the good news, Albert."

Albert looked genuinely abashed at this point. "It's . . . nothing really."

Kay stamped her foot in disbelief. "Albert? I don't believe you. Nothing?" she linked her arm with his. "Here's 'nothing', Benny: he sold a novel to Gnome Press."

"That's a pretty big nothing," Benny said. "Gnome Press. Congratulations! Robots?"

Albert smiled, in spite of his shyness. "What else," he said. "It's called 'Infrastructure.'" He paused. "I think that it might be the first of three volumes."

Benny slapped his friend on the back. Life was good. This was all very good. There had been pain in the past, but things were working out, and he could build on that, he could take his dreams and turn them into something more substantial.

Suddenly, with a sound like a thunderclap, the door was flung open. Pabst stood there, empty-handed, looking somehow shrunken and swollen at the same time. He stared at them all accusingly, as if their very joy was somehow an affront.

Julius was oblivious to his mood. "It's about time," he said.

Pabst didn't answer him.

"Hey, Douglas," Herbert smiled. "Where's the magazine?"

Pabst opened his hands and held them out, emphasizing their emptiness. "There *is* no magazine," he said. He chose his words deliberately, with the care of a biologist moving a pathogen from one petri dish to another. "Not this month, anyway. Mister Stone had the entire run pulped."

Benny was dumbstruck. He felt as if every one of those words had smashed into his chest like a wrecking ball. All of his carefully constructed fantasies just seemed to wilt. "What?" he whispered. "He can't do that?"

Pabst glared at him, but there was something unutterably sad at the very back of his eyes. Something scared and lost, immediately covered up with a patina of anger. "He can and he did," Pabst said. "He believes that this issue quote, 'did not meet our usual high standards,' unquote."

The very air in the room felt as if it was frozen. "And just what is that supposed to mean?" Russell asked.

"It means," Pabst said as if explaining fire to a schoolchild, "that he didn't like it."

Pabst walked heavily to the window and gazed out of it, down into the street, his hands and arms seemed to work almost independently, pouring him a cup of coffee. He seemed to want to put the whole thing behind him. "It means," he said, warming to his subject, "that the public's simply going to have to get along without *Incredible Tales of Scientific Wonder* this month."

The silence tore at Benny as if it would eat him alive if he didn't hear the truth. "Douglas," he said. Anger boiled in his veins like lava, "you still haven't said what he didn't like. The artwork? The layout? Exactly what 'high standards' is he talking about?" His voice was rising, and he hated the sound of it, hoped that it wouldn't break before he had a chance to get it all out.

He looked down and realized that his hands were balled into fists.

He felt a gentle touch on his arm and snapped his head around, almost not recognizing Kay. "Take it easy, Benny," she urged.

But he couldn't. This was just too much, too

infuriating, was cutting too deeply into his tattered pride. He felt something breaking inside him. Not just breaking, but shattering.

He took a deep breath. "It's about my story, isn't it? That's what this is all about. He didn't want to publish my story, and we all know why." His fists drummed against his legs rhythmically, and he had a terrible, almost aching need to hit something. "It's because my hero is a colored man."

Pabst's eyes seemed to have retreated behind shells of glass. "Hey. Mister Stone owns this magazine. If he doesn't want to publish this month—we don't publish this month. End of story."

Benny felt that blackness boiling behind his eyes again. "That doesn't make it right, and you know it."

Pabst squinted. "Don't tell me what I know. Besides, it's not about what's right. It's about what *is.*" He took a deep breath, like a man steeling himself for a mighty effort, and laid the rest of his cards on the table. "I'm afraid I have some more bad news for you, Benny. Mister Stone has decided your services are no longer required here."

The others were taken aback, and looked at Benny as if afraid that this blow would crumble him, but instead, the announcement only seemed to fuel his anger. "You're firing me?" Benny asked.

"I have no choice, Benny," he said. "It's his decision."

"Well, you can't fire me," Benny said. "I quit. To hell with Stone and to hell with you."

Julius looked downright alarmed. "Try to stay calm," he said.

Herbert, Albert, and Julius came up alongside Benny, sensing that it might be a good idea for them to get between him and Pabst.

"Calm, Benny," Herbert repeated in what he must have hoped was a soothing voice.

"I'm tired of being calm," Benny said. "Calm's never gotten me a damned thing."

The sheer blast of fury from Benny was something that none of them had ever seen. And Pabst, clearly, was taken aback. This was not the calm, intelligent but malleable Benny he was used to. "I'm warning you, Benny—if you don't stop shouting, I'm calling the cops."

Benny's hands opened, and then clinched again, and then hooked into claws. His voice dropped to an ugly rasp. "Call them," Benny snarled. "Go ahead. They can't do anything to me. Not anymore." He looked around the room as if he was looking at strangers and they looked back at him, realizing that in core, key ways that they hadn't let themselves consider, had never let themselves consider, Benny was a stranger to all of them. "None of you can," he said.

Herbert reached out for him again, but Benny broke away. Everyone stepped back. They had no idea what he might do next—and knew only that they didn't want him to do it to them.

Benny stood in the middle of the room, alone, his fists clinched. He made no move to step toward them, gave no indication that he wanted to hurt. No, he was the one hurting. He was the one who was damaged. There would be no shattered furniture or broken bones. The anger began to fade, and they saw beneath it the fear and loneliness of a man who had worked long and hard to earn their company, and now understood that he had never truly had it.

"I'm a human being, god dammit!" he said. He fought to hold the emotions back, but they burst out of him like a dark, muddy torrent. And caught in that morass were the reflections of stars. So many. So beautiful. So impossibly distant. "I . . . *exist.*"

He paused, and seemed almost to be listening, as if to some music that only he could hear. "You can deny me all you want but you can't deny Ben Sisko. He lives!" His eyes were defocused, locked, lost on some faraway point, some place beyond their time, a world on the other side of the universe. "He lives," Benny whispered. "That space station . . . those people . . . that future . . . they exist!" He pointed to his head with one trembling brown finger. "In here," he said. "And in every one of you that read it."

They said nothing, and Benny blinked. They stood before him, but simultaneously, almost as if superimposed over them, were the forms of the others, the characters that he had cloaked them with in his story. Major Kira. Quark. The others. They were all there, waiting to be born, calling to him. They were real. *This* was fantasy.

"You hear what I'm telling you?" he whispered hoarsely. "You can pulp the story but you can't destroy the idea." He blinked hard. Where was he? In the offices, or . . . where? "That future is real," he said, but he took a step backwards, and wavered, as if that outburst, those words, this walk to the office, perhaps that story itself had extracted some essence from Benny Russell, and without it, he might no longer live at all. As if the story he had told were more real than he. "I made it real!" he raised his voice, until he was almost screaming. Spittle flew from his mouth. "It's real!" he screamed again. The two words were some kind of desperate magical incantation, a final, futile attempt to keep the story, his dream, those thousands of pulped magazines alive.

"It's *REAL!*" The last word became a sustained howl, one that must have split his throat, one that pierced the air, pierced their brains, a howl of rage, and pain and loss that echoed on and on and spoke of death, and hopelessness, and worst of all, betrayal.

CHAPTER
37

A CROWD HAD GATHERED at the front door of the Arthur Trill Building. An ambulance with a white cross painted on its side waited there, its back doors hanging open.

Slowly, without haste, in fact with an almost funereal calm, two ambulance orderlies emerged from the building pulling a stretcher.

Strapped to the stretcher was a Negro man whose hand and feet twitched like a dreaming dog's, a man whose eyes stared sightlessly at the sky, whose face was infused with some terrible mixture of wonder and fear.

He could not speak, had nothing to say to the people who gazed at him, wondering what strange mixture of alcohol and drugs might have reduced him to such a state.

There was something surreal about the scene. Something unnaturally quiet. And for Benny, he could see their mouths move, but could not hear them, almost as if he was separated from them by a sheet of glass. He heard . . .

Nothing. Who was he? And who were they? And where was this strange and wondrous place that he had found himself?

The two ambulance orderlies carried him into the back of the vehicle, and then sat, staring at each other, moving in perfect synchrony, as if this were an action that they had rehearsed many, many times.

They did not look at him. They did not speak.

They merely stared straight ahead into each other's faces, like an odd mirror image.

The back of the ambulance opened, and a man stepped in. Benny felt the weight as the springs sagged, felt the shadow looming over him. The two attendants didn't seem to notice. Nor did the driver, who began to ease out into traffic.

Tied to the stretcher, Benny blinked hard and looked up at the newcomer, recognizing him even in the upside-down configuration. The Preacher.

He sat next to Benny, laying a comforting hand on his shoulder. He smiled, and the smile was comforting; it was, in fact, an expression of profound respect, the affection of one warrior for another. "Rest, Brother Benny," the Preacher said. "This is but one battle in a war that started long ago, and will continue long after you're gone."

Benny closed his eyes. Against the blackness of his

inner lids, stars shone like jewels. He opened them again, and lay his head to the side, looking down at his body. His suit had disappeared. He recognized the uniform he wore. It was Ben Sisko's Starfleet dress uniform. Medals shone upon his chest, medals he had won in another place and time for valor under fire. For courage in the face of the enemy.

The Preacher smiled. "Don't despair," he said. "You've walked in the path of the Prophets. There's no greater glory."

His eyes focused on a red and purple rectangle of cloth and gilt. What was that ribbon? He thought he recognized it. It was Bajoran, and rare as a black pearl. It was given for courage, and the risk of life, in the winning of a great and lasting peace.

He felt an odd calm stealing over him. *If this is death,* he thought, *then I will not resist it.* But he knew that that was not it, either. Then if it was not his life, and it was not death either, then what?

Benny didn't know. He looked back up at the Preacher. "Tell me, please," he said. "Who am I?"

"Don't you know?" the Preacher said.

Quite quietly, without any fuss, the ambulance drivers were fading away. Before they vanished, they smiled. The walls of the ambulance dissolved, and in the gaps there was only a vast and silent expanse of stars.

"Tell me!" he cried, confused but already sensing the answer.

He looked around, but he was alone. There was

nothing but Benny, and the infinite stellar display. Then, out of that void, came the Preacher's voice. Comforting, eternal.

"You are the dreamer," the Preacher said. *"And the Dream."*

SHUFFLE

CHAPTER
38

BENJAMIN SISKO opened his eyes, blinking against the light of *Deep Space Nine*'s sterile infirmary walls. *Where? What?*

Bashir. Kasidy. Joseph Sisko. Jake. All were right there, waiting, their eyes anxious. He was back in his own world—if he could truly call it that.

Kasidy Yates threw her arms around him, her lovely brown face taut with concern. "Ben!" she cried, her voice ragged. "Thank God!"

Sisko struggled to sit up, and she tried to help him. He wasn't quite strong enough to do it, and ended up back on his elbows, shaking his head in a vain attempt to clear it. "What happened?" he asked.

Doctor Bashir approached him, scanning with a tricorder in an attempt to get a reading. "You slipped into a coma," he said. He looked calm, but Sisko knew that beneath that practiced exterior churned a sea of emotions.

"How long was I out?" Sisko asked.

"Only a few minutes," Bashir said.

"Seemed like forever to me," Joseph Sisko said soberly.

Bashir stared at the tricorder's readout panel, puzzled and fascinated. "That's interesting."

"What is it?" Sisko asked.

"Somehow, your neural patterns have returned to normal."

Jake grinned with relief. "That's good, isn't it?"

"It's very good," Bashir said. "I just don't understand how it happened."

"Well, doctor," Sisko said, feeling greater strength flowing back into his body with every moment. "Let's not inspect our gift horses too carefully, shall we? We should take our miracles where we find them."

CHAPTER
39

THE *RAKTAJINO* WAS EXCELLENT, every sip worth savoring. Sisko stood by the window in his quarters, staring out at the stars, quietly enjoying the moment and Kasidy's company.

They had spoken of several things, but he knew that Kasidy had been circling, circling around some subject that she was as yet afraid to approach directly.

Soon, she would no longer avoid it.

The stars . . . he thought. I've seen them so many times. Why do I feel that I have never seen them at all?

"There's one thing I still don't understand," Kasidy said, finally breaking the silence between them, as he had known she would have to do.

He smiled. "Just one?"

"For the moment." She paused. "If what you experienced was another vision from the Prophets—what was it they were trying to tell you?"

Indeed, he had thought on this himself. What could he say? They had—mostly—agreed that the abnormal neural patterns had been caused by an induced vision, but what to make of all of this?

He chose his words very carefully. "At first," he said, "I thought it was their way of reminding me how far the human race has come, that however dark things might seem, they used to be a hell of a lot worse."

He paused. "But then I started wondering . . . ," his voice trailed off.

"Wondering what?" she asked.

He seemed about to answer when the door chimed. "Come in," Sisko said without looking over.

It opened and Joseph Sisko entered. With grave courtliness he kissed Kasidy's hand, then studied his son's face.

"How're you feeling, Son?"

"Okay."

"Are you leaving now, Joseph?" Kasidy asked.

"I'm done packing," he said. "Transport leaves at eight in the morning."

"I wish you could stay longer," she said. "We're just getting acquainted."

"There'll be another time. I've got to get back to the restaurant. My customers have never gone this long without me."

Benjamin thought about his father's cooking, and another sudden longing swept him. To have had the time for one of his father's elegant yet simple culinary masterpieces . . . that was a gift he would give himself, and soon. *Time passes so quickly,* he thought. Treasure the gifts you are given. Like family.

And like the magnificent woman who had stolen his heart.

His father was still watching him, his expression faintly humorous. "The question is, son—what are *you* going to do?"

"The only thing I can do," he said. "Stay here and finish the job I started. And if I fail . . . at least I'll go down fighting."

" 'I have fought the good fight,' " Joseph quoted. " 'I have finished the course. I have kept the faith.' "

Sisko squinted at his father, startled. "I've never known you to quote scripture."

"Just full of surprises, aren't I?" He paused. "And so are you. It sounds like this dream you had helped you sort things out."

"I suppose it did. But I've been wondering . . . what if it wasn't a dream?" he said. "What if this life we're leading . . . all of this . . . you and me . . . everything . . . what if it's all an illusion?"

Her mouth opened, and then closed again. Kasidy stared into his face as if searching for reassurances, and failed to find them. "You're starting to scare me, Ben."

He smiled, and squeezed her hand tightly. He nodded. "I'm scaring myself a bit. But maybe, just maybe, Benny isn't the dream—we are." He thought about that, and liked it. It had symmetry. "Perhaps, we're nothing more than figments of *his* imagination."

Benjamin Sisko looked out at the stars, and as he did, the wormhole opened again. A tiny freighter darted out, carrying what cargo? From where? He assumed they existed, yet he saw only the shell of a craft, and from that his mind had extrapolated a home planet, and lives, families, fates.

All from a momentary glimpse.

In a moment, he had tasted the entire life and hopes and aspirations of a man completely different from him, and yet . . .

And yet the same. How dare he assume that man might not exist? Or perhaps they both existed in different times, in different worlds, but through the gift of the

(Preacher)

Prophets, each had been given a momentary glimpse of the other. A blessing? A curse? Who could ever say such a thing. All of life is both, and neither.

"Ben?" Kasidy asked, still peering up into his face.

"For all we know," Sisko said, "at this very moment, somewhere, far beyond all those stars, Benny Russell is dreaming of us."

He slipped an arm around Kasidy and stood with two of the human beings he loved most in all the world. He thought of Cassie. And of the Preacher. And of their very different, oddly similar gifts of faith.

Benjamin Sisko gazed out at the stars, and remembered Manhattan skies. His reflection, glimpsed briefly in the window, was of another man, from another time. A simpler man, but no less complex. A man who fought no world-spanning battles, but a warrior nonetheless.

Benny Russell lives, he thought. *As long as I remember him, he lives.*

And perhaps as long as he remembers me, I live as well.

the latter half of the twentieth century. There is so much to love here—but also much to be disappointed with. I was born in 1952, and if there is any most central reason I began to write, it is that there was no father in my home, and I needed to find images of men doing manly stuff. My mom did the best she could but she was (very much) a woman, and simply couldn't teach me certain things. So I looked to the stories of Conan the Barbarian, and Mike Hammer, and James Bond, and Leslie Charteris's the Saint. And there was something very interesting about all of these he-man worlds: no black people needed apply.

It was positively grotesque. When Edgar Rice Burroughs wrote that "White men have imagination, Negroes have little, animals have none," he was doubtless merely expressing the attitudes of the time. That didn't make it any easier to read, and I would have put that Tarzan novel down if I hadn't so desperately needed the emotional vitamins within. True, as Kay Bass rightly points out, there aren't enough female characters with spunk and grit, but girls aren't required to "prove" themselves in aggressive, violent competition in order to be considered "feminine." Little black boys and little white boys want pretty much the same things out of life, across the board, and most of what we do in life, we learn from watching role models.

Don't believe it? You learned to walk and talk and ride bicycles by watching others do it. Shouldn't black children be able to learn by watching white heroes, you say? Well, obviously—and yet the more levels of logical abstraction between you and the role model, the more difficult it is to empathize. Trust me, sit in a Hollywood pitch meeting, and watch the executives try to sandwich a white character into a black story, parroting the wisdom that "audiences won't identify." And what happens if they don't? Why, the accepted, hard-learned wisdom is that they won't go into the theaters.

Well, come the 1960s or so, and black characters began appearing in science fiction, horror, and action films. But do you know what? They usually existed only to die horribly, and usually to protect white people. (And whatever feminists say about the parallels between sexism and racism, there is *no* similar pattern of women dying in movies to protect men. Quite the opposite, in fact. Male lives are cheaper than women's, and minority lives cheaper than white.)

The list of films using these nauseating images unfortunately encompasses some of Hollywood's best. The following is a very partial list of movies which contained a 100% black fatality rate, often in the noble protection of the white lead: *The Alamo, Spartacus, Full Metal Jacket, The Dirty Dozen, Alien I, II,* and *III,* any James Cameron film . . .

Oh, Jeeze, the list goes on and on. Just in the last year or so we've had *Daylight, Mimic, Starship Troopers* and *Alien IV.* It gets hard. It was to the point when, as a kid, I would go see some SF flick with a black character and when I returned home the other kids in the neighborhood would ask: "Well, how did they kill the Brother this time?"

Poor Paul Winfield actually made a career out of

dying in SF movies. *Wrath of Khan* (protecting William Shatner), *Terminator* (protecting Linda Hamilton), *Serpent and the Rainbow* (protecting Bill Pullman) and, most insultingly, in *Damnation Alley*. Oh, I remember watching *that* movie. In fact, I'll never forget it. Here's George Peppard, Jan Michael Vincent, and Paul Winfield traveling across a nuclear devastated landscape in a souped-up Winnebago. Suddenly, out of the wreckage of a bombed-out city crawls—Dominique Sanda. Possibly the last woman in the world. Very, very white.

I turned to my date, and said: "Oh nuts—they're going to kill Paul Winfield." She said: "Why?" I said, "Because they can't pretend he won't be interested in her, and they're not going to let him compete for her."

My date, who was white, thought this was incredibly cynical of me. Five minutes later, Paul Winfield got eaten by giant roaches.

Memories are made of this.

But cinematic reality has shifted, and continues to change so rapidly that I can hardly keep up with things anymore. Most notably, this was signaled when *Independence Day,* starring Will Smith, made money faster than Bill Gates. I still remember seeing it at the Cinedome theater in Castle Rock, Washington. The parking lot was filled with pickup trucks sporting rebel flags—not exactly a hotbed of NAACP supporters if you know what I mean, and I think you do. Anyway, after the film I went to the men's room, and as I stood in line at the urinal, I saw a bunch of good ol' boys heeding the call of nature and yacking up a storm to each other, quote: "whoo-eee! That Will Smith was he, like, too cool, or what? I'm bringin' my Daddy back here tomorrow. He's gotta see this!"

Damn, I thought—what planet am I on?

Television has been a tougher nut to crack than motion pictures, at least partially because a show needs so many tens of millions of viewers just to survive. The reality is that it took over forty years for television to produce and sustain even one single dramatic television series with a non-Caucasian star. Oh, there are plenty of comedies—the modern equivalent of *Amos and Andy* shows. Too damned many of them, if you ask me. And blacks or Asians have had plenty of "second billing" success—costars, supporting roles, you name it.

But not heroes. Not first-billed. Except . . .

Well, I'm getting ahead of myself.

The first chink in the cultural armor was a triple-assault, two of them launched by the same small company, a place called Desilu. The most talked about was probably 1965's *I Spy,* with Bill Cosby costarring with Robert Culp. God, I loved that show. Here was a black man who was articulate, literate, and funny—and he could break your face. Yow!

But the next year in October of 1966, we had Greg Morris on *Mission Impossible*. He played Barney Collier, who was clearly the most competent member of the entire Imposible Missions Force. After all—he could break heads, do impersonations, crack computers, or plan missions. The man had everything.

A little earlier that same year, a beautiful young woman named Nichelle Nichols stepped in front of the camera on another Desilu stage, this time for an unheralded space opera called *Star Trek*. Even though relegated to the background, she was there, a recognizable human being of intelligence and courage, and I felt proud. Gene Roddenberry knew that black people would exist in the future, and he put his money where his mouth was.

Television played with the concept of ethnicity for the next few decades. They tried several times to give blacks or Asians their own series, but the audience voted with their TV sets, and not one of them lasted longer than a season. America wasn't ready, and Hollywood was flushing its dollars down the toilet even to try.

And then came *Deep Space Nine*. Here it is, kids, the point of this entire essay, the reason why I worked like a maniac to finish this book by a deadline that would have intimidated Sisyphus—*Deep Space Nine* is, in my opinion, a major cultural turning point for America, and therefore, the world as a whole. Like it or not, the truth is that the entire world marches to our cultural beat. No one can produce mythic images like America, and myths, shared myths, are what make a culture.

Television is the connective tissue of the world's emerging culture, and don't *ever* underestimate its power.

DS9 is, as far as I am concerned, the first successful dramatic television show in history with a non-

Caucasian star. People have pointed out *Room 222* with Lloyd Haynes, and *Julia* with Diahann Carroll. Both lasted more than two seasons, and so should be considered successes, but they were borderline comedies, and just don't count.

But *Deep Space Nine* . . .

Ah, Sisko. Soft-spoken but commanding. Nurturing but virile. Intuitive but brilliant. In the hands of the protean Avery Brooks, *Deep Space Nine* is, in its quiet way, as important as anything that has ever happened in the history of entertainment.

And it could never have succeeded without the millions of die-hard *Star Trek* fans who have loyally supported that series, and its spin-offs, through the decades.

I have heard (and occassionally made) jokes at the expense of those who love Gene Roddenberry's dream. But let me tell you, people. It is not easy for human beings to look at those of other cultures, races, or genders and recognize their own humanity. It has *never* been easy. For years, science fiction fans said that our field trains us to do this, to see the heart hidden within the alien form. But, apparently, only as long as a white guy was wearing the costume. Then, for the first time, with DS9, that dream of a universal empathy came true. And, I believe, because of it, we got films like *Independence Day*—a silly piece of fluff, to be sure, but the very first film in history to take seriously the old adage that "if the aliens showed up, we earthlings would drop our differences." I can tear that film up as well as anyone—but I'll tell you honestly that I sat in the theater with tears rolling down my cheeks, wishing to God that I had seen that movie when I was nine. And thanking heaven that my daughter was growing up in a better world than mine.

And when I first saw DS9—in fact when I first heard that Avery Brooks had been cast, I was so terribly afraid that it would fail, that it would join the long, long line of Neilsen disasters that had littered the electronic landscape my whole life . . . and when the legions of *Star Trek* fans supported it with their whole hearts, and gave it a chance to find its rhythm and create its own niche.

I was so proud of the field I have loved since childhood. I have *never* been as grateful to be a part of the community called fandom. You came through, guys. You walked the talk.

I love being alive in the nineties. You folks give me hope.

So, early November I was heading out my front door with a copy of my new novel *Iron Shadows* under my arm, when the telephone rang. It was my agent, the lovely, charming and ruthless Eleanor Wood, who said that John Ordover at Pocket Books had specifically requested me to write a very special DS9 novel, and would I be interested?

I have to tell you honestly—there is *no* other show I would have done this for. I wrote it as a way of saying "thank you," to the millions of fans who helped to change the face of America, and the world; to the show's creators Rick Berman and Michael Piller, who took a chance; to Marc Scott Zicree, Ira Steven Behr, and Hans Beimler, the creators of an extraordinary script; and to a man no longer with us, the singular Gene Roddenberry, who saw what had to be done, and did it.

I love you all. Thanks, guys.

Steven Barnes
Vancouver, Washington
www.teleport.com/~djuru
lifewrite@aol.com

About the Author

Steven Barnes has published fourteen novels, among them the bestselling *Dream Park* (with Larry Niven), *Legacy of Heorot* and *Beowulf's Children* (with both Niven and Jerry Pournelle). His solo novels include *Streetlethal, Gorgon Child, Firedance, The Kundalini Equation,* and *Blood Brothers.* He was creative consultant on the full-length animated film *Secret of NIMH.* His television work includes episodes of *The Twilight Zone, The Real Ghostbusters, Stargate, The Wizard,* and *Baywatch.* He has been nominated for the Hugo and Cable Ace Awards, and is the writer of "A Stitch In Time," the Emmy-winning episode of Showtime's *The Outer Limits.*

His newest novel, *Iron Shadows,* is available from Tor Books.

Look for STAR TREK Fiction from Pocket Books

Star Trek®: The Original Series

Star Trek: The Next Generation®

Star Trek: Deep Space Nine®

Star Trek®: Voyager™

Flashback • Diane Carey
The Black Shore • Greg Cox
Mosaic • Jeri Taylor

#1 *Caretaker* • L. A. Graf
#2 *The Escape* • Dean W. Smith & Kristine K. Rusch
#3 *Ragnarok* • Nathan Archer
#4 *Violations* • Susan Wright
#5 *Incident at Arbuk* • John Greggory Betancourt
#6 *The Murdered Sun* • Christie Golden
#7 *Ghost of a Chance* • Mark A. Garland & Charles G.
  McGraw
#8 *Cybersong* • S. N. Lewitt
#9 *Invasion #4: The Final Fury* • Dafydd ab Hugh
#10 *Bless the Beasts* • Karen Haber
#11 *The Garden* • Melissa Scott
#12 *Chrysalis* • David Niall Wilson
#13 *The Black Shore* • Greg Cox
#14 *Marooned* • Christie Golden
#15 *Echoes* • Dean W. Smith & Kristine K. Rusch

Star Trek®: New Frontier

#1 *House of Cards* • Peter David
#2 *Into the Void* • Peter David
#3 *The Two-Front War* • Peter David
#4 *End Game* • Peter David
#5 *Martyr* • Peter David

Star Trek®: Day of Honor

Book One: Ancient Blood • Diane Carey
Book Two: Armageddon Sky • L. A. Graf
Book Three: Her Klingon Soul • Michael Jan Friedman
Book Four: Treaty's Law • Dean W. Smith & Kristine K. Rusch